PROJECT CHARON 2: ORIGINATOR

PATTY JANSEN

GET FREE EBOOKS

Visit pattyjansen.com
to sign up for Patty's mailing list. You get four series starter
ebooks for free!

DID YOU KNOW?

Project Charon 2: Originator is also available in audio. Click the image or visit https://pattyjansen.com to find out more.

CHAPTER ONE

"YOU DECIDE," Finn said. "This is your ship."

He leaned back in his chair aboard the habitat of the private vessel *Alethia,* which had just exited a jump and now hurtled through dark space awaiting instructions about where to jump next.

Instructions the vessel's captain, Tina Freeman, mother, ex-Federacy Force scientist and fugitive was about to give. If she could get her only adult human passenger to advise her sensibly on the two available choices.

"No, I asked for your opinion. I know what I prefer, but it's based on fifteen-year old information. Is it still current?"

Tina spread her hands in frustration. Ever since it had become clear that the presence of extra unplanned passengers on board would necessitate them stopping somewhere and resupplying the ship, Finn had been evasive.

Neither of the two eligible stations were particularly safe or desirable. They were both in the hands of pirates, or Freerangers as they liked to call themselves. Neither had an established Federacy Force presence, and both were the subject of unsavoury rumours, which, in case of at least one of the stations, were true.

Finn protested. "I don't know much either. When I was on the Federacy Force ships, we never came to these types of stations. And besides, I was only a ship engineer, and responsibility for deciding where to dock was way above my rank."

"I know. I was in the Force, too, remember?" She tried not to let her frustration show, but found that hard to do. "But you still know more than any of us about how welcoming and safe these stations are likely to be."

This discussion was going around in circles, and had been doing that since she started it.

She had asked, again and again, for his opinion, and he had managed to twist the discussion around to a different subject on every occasion and now they were out of time and a decision needed to be made.

"Well, we have two options. We have Beta Station, which is probably slightly closer, but has always had a rather unsavoury reputation. For one, it's the place where a lot of sordid sex trafficking went on when I was in the Force. I've been there so I know that to be true. But that was a very long time ago and things may have changed."

"A little bit," Finn said. "It's not as bad as it used to be, but that sort of thing is very hard to stamp out."

He sounded half-hearted about it, which probably meant not much had changed. As a man, he probably wouldn't care as much, but she remembered the warnings female Force members were given before their troop carrier docked at the station on the way to Pandana. Avoid leaving the ship. If you have to leave, always go in groups. If someone accosts you, politely decline anything they offer. The list was long.

Tina continued, "And we obviously don't want any of us to face any trouble in that department."

This was mostly about Rasa, the stray girl they had picked up on Kelso Station and whose presence, and that of her five geese, was unplanned. She was a smart enough kid, the same age as Tina's son Rex. The two sat at the table, taking apart the rear airlock control panel to see if they could cannibalise and repurpose some of the parts for a lock on the door in the cabin that held Rasa's five geese so that they would no longer be accidentally released into the rest of the ship at inopportune moments.

Geese and weightlessness were not a good combination.

"The other option is Aurora Station," Tina continued. "It's very big and has a large independent economy."

"Which is now in pirate hands,' Finn said.

"Yes, but so is Beta. Aurora has a native population of more than a million. Those people are still going to be at the station, and a lot of business is still going to continue as usual. They're taking ships, the docks are open to all vessels and the cargo ports are open."

Finn snorted. "Of course they are. They have to eat."

"A large population means that there will be plenty of civilians to hide behind," Tina said. "It's easier to hide in a bigger station where you don't stand out because of your gender."

"The pirates are in control. How stable is the station going to be? What are we going to do if we get swamped by refugees?"

"Who says that's going to happen?" She was growing really tired of his subject-changing.

"I've seen it happen," Finn said. He met Tina's eyes. "It's not pretty when it does and no one can do anything about it once the masses in a station start to panic and decide they want off. If a ship turns up, the ship and the crew have had it."

Tina had been going to say something about him avoiding answering the question, but she had heard about refugees swamping arriving ships, too. Stories had circulated of stations that were taken over by pirates, where all the residents flocked to the docks and utter chaos broke out so that the station authorities could no longer control the crowds. Ship crew were lynched, people crushed to death, ships cast off only to crash into a part of the station in the hands of unskilled pilots. Or disappear never to be heard from again.

A chill came over her.

"Beta is under pirate control, too," Tina reminded him. "The same could happen there. If there was a nearby station that wasn't under pirate control, I'd go there, but we don't have that option. Both options are less than ideal."

"I want to go to Aurora," Rex said.

Tina turned back to him, catching a glimpse out the window of the part of the ship that contained the controls. The habitat was at the end of one of two long beams that rotated constantly to give the passengers the semblance of gravity.

"Why do you want to go to Aurora?" she asked. But she thought she already knew: so that he could spend more money on gadgets. Wasn't it funny she was out of cash but he still had all his pocket money saved up?

Rex flicked the magnifying lens he'd been using back into the top of the breastplate of his harness.

"Jens lives there," he said.

"And Jens is...?" She had trouble keeping all his friends straight. They were all from the many forums that Rex frequented. Rex mentioned them sometimes, but Tina had no idea who they were or where they lived.

"Jens is the one who suggested that if we wanted the recycler to run more efficiently, we install the filter upside down and run the fan exhaust through the ice chamber twice. He can show us how to fix the inverter."

That sounded attractive. Power supply in the habitat had been a constant battle that limped from one stopgap solution to the next. Tina swore she knew the ship so well because she'd been forced to find her way in the dark half the time. When the damn thing wasn't working, Finn would give priority to the ventilation, since it kept them alive, and he and Rex would spend hours examining the habitat's wiring to see why the thing kept crapping out, usually with Rasa holding up the emergency light.

She could write a long list of "don'ts" based on this trip, but the top one would be: don't take a ship that's been sitting unused in dock for fifteen years on a long interplanetary flight. The memory of that first time the ship almost missed the jump window because the phase alternator wanted to update its software was still etched in her mind.

Fixing the ship up properly sounded really good, especially since this friend Jens sounded like a capable mechanic. Being a friend might also entitle her to a cheaper rate, since her utter lack of funds was also going to catch up with them as soon as they came back into anything that resembled civilisation.

Finn, well-trained as he was as ship engineer, knew nothing about small ships. On board the behemoth Federacy Force supply ship SS *Stavanger*, his task had been to service the engines that ran coolant through the shell around the ship's fusion chamber. Lacking a fusion chamber, the *Alethia*'s ion drive had stumped him with its "crude simplicity", as he said.

Which Tina had learned to interpret as a translation for "I have no idea how it works".

Finn didn't like admitting defeat. He'd spent hours reading up. He'd gotten much better. But a broken part was still a broken part, no matter the skill of the mechanic.

"I still don't like Aurora," he said.

He had said this before, but now he was going to have to come up with a reason.

"From where I'm standing, it seems the most logical place to go of the two," Tina said. "The pirates will be less in control of a station like Aurora, because it's much bigger, and a lot of commercial flights are necessary just to keep everything running smoothly. If we're going to keep our heads down, it will be much easier if there are a lot of other heads."

"Haha."

He said nothing for a while, but sipped his synthetic coffee. It was warm and tasted vaguely like the real thing, and, frankly, after months in space, any food tasted good because it was a distraction.

"Before I make a final decision, can you tell me why you have a problem with us going to Aurora, because there is not much point in hearing this after we have already made our choice."

"I don't have a problem with going there."

"Sorry, I don't believe that. Every time I raise the subject, you try to steer us away from making the decision to go there. It's my preferred option. Rex wants to go there. We might be able to access a cheap mechanic there. What's your objection?"

Over the humming of the ship, and the regular clicks as the arm with the habitat attached swung around, she could hear the honking of geese. Those damn things kept going day and night, and you could hear them everywhere when they got going. Their home was at the end of the ship's second rotating arm. At least they provided eggs.

"It's like this," Finn finally said. "My father had some business interests at Aurora that went bad. There are some people at the station who are very sensitive to the Kaspari name."

"You don't have to go into the station and no one has to know that you're on board our ship. I'll be using my second identity. I don't think there's much of a chance that anyone finds out who we are. There are millions of people at Aurora, and our names will be just a line on the ship docket. We won't go into the station except to buy supplies and refuel, and then we'll be gone again. No one will know."

"And what about this friend who fixes inverters?"

"That's just a friend of Rex's. He's likely to be a fairly young fellow, probably someone who works in the docks or some other technical job."

"There is never 'just a friend'," Finn said. "Everyone should be treated with suspicion, even the very young or the very old, the needy or the very rich. My family's enemies have very convincing ways of getting even with people they don't like. When you have money, you attract criminals. The more money, the worse the criminals."

"Any reason why they're looking for you?"

"They're not," Finn admitted. "They don't know that I'm here. I'd like to keep it that way."

"You do have a second identity you can use?" Most higher-ranking people did, even if it was illegal.

"I do."

"Then use that, and stay on board. Problem solved."

"The site reviews say Aurora is cheaper for ship services," Rex said. "They say the cost of resupplying a ship with a standard package—whatever that means—is ten to fifteen percent lower than at nearby stations."

He was looking at the screen that folded out from his metal arm.

Tina got up from the couch. "That's it then. We're going to Aurora. I'll go and set the navigation. We can cope with unfriendly locals. We can't cope with my severe shortage of money. I like the idea of someone being able to fix our inverter cheaply."

When she walked past him, Finn still looked unhappy.

Tina climbed the ladder into the middle of the habitat, and ascended into the arm that attached the habitat to the rest of the ship. As she climbed, she felt herself getting lighter, until she could push off and float into the control cabin, which sat atop the central cylinder that formed the ship and which contained the engines.

The lights in this part of the ship were off to conserve battery power in case of an inverter mishap.

By the bluish glow from the ship's controls, she floated over the rows of seats where the passengers sat when the habitat had to be stowed for arrival and departure.

She pulled herself into the pilot's seat and went through the motions. She checked the coordinates, entered the destination, checked the jump queue and reported her intention to visit Aurora Station.

Sector Control came back with permission and a time slot when they would open a jump window. Tina made note of it and intended to be at the controls at least an hour before, to check if everything worked.

But first, there was time for dinner.

Honestly, she was looking forward to having something other than curry with goose eggs. So many things had already run out. It was high time they resupplied the ship.

CHAPTER TWO

WHEN TINA CAME BACK into the habitat, the couch was empty.

"Where is Finn?" she asked.

"He said he was going to the gym," Rex said.

The gym was in the other swinging arm of the habitat section, and accessible only through the zero-gravity centre of the ship. She hadn't noticed anyone coming past when she was at the controls, but the tube was at the back of the passage, and she had been busy.

"He seems so grumpy," Rex said.

"Yeah, I'm not sure what's going on," Tina said. She stood behind Rex, looking at the little parts that Rex and Rasa had taken out of the airlock panel that lay on the table, labelled and numbered so that they could remember what went where. The collection of little chips wobbled slightly with the constant movement of the habitat's rotation.

"You really didn't want to go to Beta," Rex said.

"I've been there. It's a foul, disgusting place. I doubt pirate occupation has made it any better. It's not safe for us."

"It's OK to say that it's about me," Rasa said, without looking up from her work.

They had turned up the light above the table to its maximum strength, which made Rasa's skin look near-white. The tiny tattoo on her upper arm stood out black.

Rasa had told her that she'd been given the mark "when I was a young girl" but had said very little about the circumstances in which she had received it. Tina had tried to search for the meaning of the small rune-like sign that looked like a satellite dish pointing upwards, but had drawn a blank.

Yet it had to mean something, most likely ownership by a pimp.

"Well," Tina said. "I wouldn't want your old life to catch up with you."

Rasa didn't reply to that. Exactly what that old life of hers was remained a mystery.

She met Rex's eyes across the table. The corner of his mouth twitched, while he used his metal hands to pull another chip loose from the circuit board.

Having Rasa along had been good for both her and Rex. Rasa was smarter than Tina would have given the dirty creature she'd first found living inside her long-abandoned ship credit for. She had expected to have to teach her to do the most basic things like clean her teeth and sleep in a bed, let alone things like reading and writing.

But to her surprise, Rasa had basic knowledge of most of those things, even if she was still scared of the noise made by the jets hissing water vapour into the shower.

Under her dirty stolen clothing, she had worn a belt with a satchel that contained a few treasures and an ID card in the name of Rasa Vichenko, with a photo of a young girl.

The name itself didn't register any warnings, but the

number matched up with the accessible part of the database and the birth date was roughly accurate. It showed Rasa as having been born at a place called Malan Intersect Station, which Tina was utterly unfamiliar with but turned out to be a medium-size industrial station in the Centauri Mining belt. Her parents were Dom Vichenko and Lara Petrova. They were both miners.

Rasa claimed that she had a brother in the Force. A Force membership search under Vichenko had brought up twenty-five records. The public side of the database didn't allow users to view the details and images of the employees.

Rasa said his name was Jack. There was no Jack in the list.

At some point the family must have broken up. If Rasa's timeline about this was correct, it had happened when she was a little girl, after which she and her mother had drifted from ship to ship, station to station, courtesy of a number of her mother's dubious boyfriends, before Rasa either ran away or was kicked out of a ship by one of those men. Her story on this varied, but in all versions it happened when she was ten.

Rasa didn't like talking about how she had survived, and Tina didn't press her. But it was frustrating sometimes.

Tina started making dinner, while Rex and Rasa finished up and packed all the bits away.

"How did you do?" Tina asked.

"We need to buy a few things to make it work," Rex said.

Why didn't that surprise her? "All I want is a simple lock on the gate so that it can't be opened accidentally."

"Yes, but that won't happen without the lock hardware. We have spare controllers, but we need a different lock."

"We need a lot of things before we can afford that. We'll just have to make do and remind everyone not to open the gate to the goose cage in zero g, or they'll get to clean the entire cabin of goose poo and feather fluff."

Rex and Rasa went off to reinstall the lock in the cargo hold in the other end of the arm that held the living areas. Their laughing and chatting was audible all the way up the ladder.

Tina liked how they got along so well. That friendly relationship had taken the tension off disagreements between her and Finn many times.

Finn now came back, his hair wet from the shower. He went to put the cups and plates on the table without saying a word.

He'd been doing this a lot recently, where he used to be quite chatty. In fact, she had only asked him to come because he seemed lonely and she could use an engineer. She had soon found out about his infamous family, though he said little about them other than that he'd signed up to the Force to escape them, only to be forcefully retired from the Force for disagreeing with a superior on a matter of safety.

She said, "Is there a problem?"

"Other than that I worry about my family's enemies catching up with me at Aurora?"

"Yes, because you've been grumpy for much longer than this."

"I'm just like that. I'm not a very cheerful person."

"You weren't like that at Kelso Station."

He replied to this with his usual silence, and it was beginning to get on Tina's nerves.

Rex and Rasa came back, filling the tense space with their laughter and chatter. They had been to feed the geese, which lived in a pen next to the gym and the farm.

They sat down at the table, and Tina brought out the ubiquitous curry with eggs that no one complained of having to eat, because there was no alternative.

"Does it mean that when we go to the station, we need to pack up everything that's in the habitats?" Rex asked.

"We do," Tina said.

Rex groaned. "What are we going to do with all this stuff?" He spread his metal hands.

"It came out of the habitat's storage, so that's where it will have to go back. We'll have a week or so to do that."

"Even the farm and your cactuses?"

Well, that was a different issue altogether. The ship consisted of a central tube that held the control cabin and the four in-flight cabins, and this ensemble sat atop the engine.

Both sides of the ship sported two swinging arms that rotated in opposite directions. The arms were attached to the ship by a central access tube, and each led to a habitat section and a cargo section. The habitat section was attached to the longest part of the arm. On one side, there was the living room, kitchen and sleeping areas. The mirror on the other side held the gym, farm and showers. The shorter arm, attached to the farm habitat, held the recycling plant and other equipment, and on the mirror side held the cargo hold. This section had an extra airlock that could be hooked up to an access tube when the ship was docked at a station.

After they had finished dinner, Tina climbed up the tube to the zero-g part of the ship and descended the other tube into the gym.

The open-plan space contained a treadmill, a bike and a few racks of pull-up and pull down machines bathed in the glow of the warm light that hung above the growth benches. The installation consisted of racks of tubing that contained constantly circulating water. Lettuce, green beans, tomatoes, mini-cucumbers, salad cabbages in different colours, strawberries and herbs grew from little holes in the tops of the tubes.

When the ship was in mid-flight, the habitat was unfolded and both sides, each with a living space and a utility space on the opposite side of the beam, could be used, but now everything that was inside the living areas needed to be packed away. Things that couldn't be packed needed to be moved to the cabins behind the control room, so that the revolving habitat could be folded for docking.

And while even the habitat was not huge, it was amazing how "not a lot of personal possessions" of four people could expand to fill the available space.

In the case of Tina's cactuses, they literally had filled the space of their own accord.

When they needed to stow the habitat, the farm had to be emptied, because otherwise the water would go everywhere in zero-g. But the cupboard at the back held a water tank that would hold the nutrient-filled water, and the installation's pipes came apart and fit neatly in the cupboard next to it. The tidiness of this ship was what had attracted Tina to buy it in the first place.

However, the prickly jungle on the far side of the room was going to be far more of a problem.

In the months of flight, while looking for something to do, Tina had grown them from the seeds she had rescued from her jacket, and they seemed to like the conditions so much that they now formed an impenetrable mass that occupied half the gym and solarium room.

Tina got off the bike and stood at the door, feeling both proud and terrified at the thought of having to move all of them. She knew that the best option was to discard them, but they reminded her of her home of so many years and symbolised Gandama in many ways: ugly, prickly, stubborn and very resilient.

Tina had put out the seeds just for fun, to remind her of home. She didn't have enough proper growth medium, because the farm didn't use it, so she used pellets from the materials recycler as anchoring substance and dried goose poo for fertiliser. Rex made up an installation of a rack of pipes with cups that held the substrate and tubes that circulated fresh air laced with nutrients over the roots. Being cactuses, they didn't need much water, and were happy with a daily spray of humid air that was supplied to the more demanding edible vegetation that took up the other half of the growth chamber. It was just that those plants, the lettuces and little tomatoes, remained neatly in their pots. The cactuses did not. They wandered all over the gym.

Several even grew handfulls of fruit—something Tina had rarely seen in her fifteen years at Gandama. They didn't appear to move quite as much as they had in her yard at Gandama, but displayed interesting growth forms Tina hadn't observed before, with one of the plants deciding to grow leaves. They were broad, waxy ones, grey-blue in colour.

She didn't want to discard them, even if she might have to lop some of them to fit into whatever space she could organise in the cabins behind the controls. There were four of those, two for sleeping and the rest for the stuff they needed to survive while the habitat was stowed and before they arrived at the station. They would have to go in with the geese.

CHAPTER THREE

TINA DIDN'T LIKE LEAVING big tasks to the last minute—and feared that if she didn't start on the cactuses now, they would run out of space and would have to discard them—so she started packing them up the next morning.

She took a large knife and cut off long fronds and other growths.

While piling them into a bucket to be incinerated, she wished she had time to perform DNA analysis on them. She had already done this during the journey, using the few simple tools she had: a kit from the onboard agriculture set, a program on her pocket reader and a handful of implements from the onboard "kitchen".

Unreliable as those results were, they appeared to confirm what she already knew: some trigger had made the plants turn on their third DNA strand that produced profoundly different growths. The ones she was putting into the bin and carting off to the incinerator were different yet again.

The plants were adapting to the surrounding space incredibly fast.

She wondered if it was Gandama that had turned the plants into cactuses, because that was the best way to guarantee survival: spikes to prevent being eaten by armadillos, leafless trunks to conserve water. It confirmed observations she had made, and would be interesting to add these latest developments to the paper that was going to be published, except it was too late for that.

When she finished cutting, she had to persuade the cactuses to sit in their pots. She needed to tie them up so that the medium didn't go floating all over the ship, and carry them up through the centre of the rotating arm into one of the cabins that was already full with far too many other supplies.

They simply had to reserve the other cabin for food and other essentials.

She floated around the cabin in zero-g, checking contents of containers to see if they really needed to be in here. For the most part, they did. During the last week of flight, they needed access to tools, spare parts for vital services, recycler filters and various cleaning products. The vacuum cleaner was definitely essential.

What was worse, they needed to build a pen in here for the geese, because she didn't want them in the cabin with the food, and although Rasa had said they could sleep in her cabin, Tina would be sleeping in the same cabin and *she* didn't want the geese in there. They never shut up.

Which meant there was less space for the cactuses, especially since the geese would probably take a bite out of them given half the chance.

And that meant she had to sort the cactuses into ones she definitely wanted to keep and ones she'd be happy to risk sticking into the cargo hold—where there was plenty of space, but it was unheated and she was afraid that the cactuses would freeze.

During all this, Finn sat at the controls. She had taught him how to operate the ship after leaving Kelso. Although he didn't have an official licence, he had flown ships before, both inside the massive maintenance halls in the Force where he didn't need a licence as long as he stayed inside, and when he was underage and still lived with his family.

Tina wanted someone else beside her capable of flying the ship well enough so that she didn't need to stay on board all the time. Also so that she had a backup pilot.

After a few trips to the gym to pick up cactuses, Rex came to join Finn by sitting in the second pilot seat, and then Rasa joined them as well. Their chatter annoyed Tina.

"Come on, we have lots of work to do."

"But mum, we're just having a break for lunch."

"No eating in here, if we can avoid it."

"I'm not eating."

"Just warning you."

"And then you say that I'm grumpy," Finn said.

"I'll quit being grumpy when the work is done."

"Yeah, yeah, we're getting to it."

Rex and Rasa pushed off from the seats behind the pilot and floated back to the tube that went into the habitat. Tina went back to the farm.

After a couple more trips she got something to eat as well, before heading up to ask if Finn wanted something. But he wasn't at the controls anymore.

Finn wasn't in the living room either.

It was strange.

Tina went back into the main body of the ship and could

hear the distinct sound of Rasa's laughter, and also Finn's voice. Then Rex gave a whoop.

What were they doing in the cargo hold? It was bitterly cold in there and they'd decided to avoid storing anything of importance there.

The cargo hold only contained the contra weights that functioned as counter-mass to stabilise any movements in the longer arm of the habitat. It also provided limited gravity, low enough to easily manoeuvre items around, but enough to keep them on the ground.

As Tina climbed out of the access hole that led into it, the pale light in the ceiling caught several glass-like objects that glittered as they flew through the air and then hit the metal deck, shattering into little pieces.

Rex called, "I win!"

Rasa laughed.

And then they fell silent, having noticed Tina.

"What's going on?" Her breath steamed. The air was bitterly cold in this space, which they only used to store those supplies that they didn't need in the near future.

Finn met her eyes. His cheeks were red from the cold. With his hands, he did up the fly of his pants.

Wait.

Tina looked from Finn to Rex.

When he still wore his old harness, Rex had been obsessed about being able to use the normal facilities, rather than wear a nappy, and he'd been especially obsessed with being able to piss standing up.

Then she looked at the glass-like fragments on the ground. Was that really what she thought it was? "I thought I was sharing this ship with adults and almost-adults. I can't believe this."

"We'll clean everything up," Finn said.

"You better."

"It's easy," Rex said. "It's so cold in here that the piss freezes before it hits the ground and you can just sweep it up."

Tina snorted.

Finn said, "Come on, every boy needs to have taken part in a pissing contest at least once. It's part of normal growing up."

Tina had a memory of the sprawling primary school building in the small agricultural community at Tirkala where she had grown up. The complex had wide spacious classrooms with wide verandas. It also included a rickety shed made of prefab panels that were light grey, but turned dark when wet. The boys were always having "who can hit the highest" contests up the wall. One day, some bright spark even got the contestants to drink dye so that it was clear who produced which wet spot. However, he hadn't figured that fluids take a while to go through the body, even of an eight-year-old boy, or realised that the dye wasn't fit for human consumption, so the day ended with a couple of boys taken to hospital for participating in a pissing contest.

She'd been about to go on a rant about immaturity, but she took a deep breath instead. Everyone had been getting along very well. She was especially happy how Rex and Rasa worked together so well. And Finn was right: a pissing contest seemed to be an essential part of boyhood that Rex had never experienced.

"Just clean it up when you're done."

"You're sure you don't want to see the results of your expensive investment in my harness?" Rex said.

"If winning a pissing contest is the best you can do then I'm not sure it was such a good investment."

"It's a pissing contest I don't have to do in a nappy anymore."

Definitely worth the exorbitant price.

Tina was only half sarcastic about that.

CHAPTER FOUR

THE *ALETHIA* EXECUTED the allocated jump perfectly. Upon checking the cabins after returning to normal space, Tina didn't even find any dislodged items.

Over the following days, the *Alethia* came closer to Aurora Station. They would only be able to see the station once they came very close, but already, the amount of traffic in the area had increased.

A station this size was a major traffic hub, even when it was occupied by pirates. People had to travel, residents were not about to leave, and there weren't enough ships in the sector to take everyone off the station anyway. So the station still needed to be supplied.

Traffic control was a major operation, and all still in the hands of the Aurora Station Authority, who, at least on the surface, appeared to know what they were doing, giving Tina details of the approach route and waiting times.

"At some point, they're going to want the names of all on board," Finn said. "I don't want the station to know that I'm on board."

"I'll give them my false identity," Tina said. She'd wanted to retire the ID, but it looked like Louise Metvier would have to do a couple more jobs.

Finn detached himself from his seat and floated over to where Tina sat. He took a small chip out of his pocket.

Tina frowned at him. "What's that?"

"When they ask our names."

Tina took the chip and put it in the reader. The identity card that came onto the screen had Finn's face, but the name of the man was David Metz, shown to be a citizen of Olympus.

"Did your family give you this?"

He nodded. "My father has several. Even my mother has them."

"Even? So mothers are worth less?"

"No, but she doesn't travel much. When she does, she usually uses her false identity to keep from being followed everywhere."

"It's so tiresome being rich and famous."

"They're not famous and didn't ask to be famous. There are lots of people with issues against our family or the company."

"I thought you were no longer employed by the company. You told me that you didn't like the way your family treated you, and wanted to go into the Force to prove yourself."

"I worked for the company up until then."

"If you use this identity, you think they won't know?"

"They will. I have no choice. If I had a third identity, I would use it. I fear what these people at Aurora might do to me, and what they might use me for to get back at my father."

"Now tell me this, I had this impression that you had fallen out with your family, and now it turns out that you're still working for them? What am I supposed to believe?"

He looked uneasy. "Once you're a Kaspari, you're always a

Kaspari, my grandfather says. No, I don't agree with many of the things they do, but they're still my family."

"And Dexter Freeman is my family, too, and he betrayed us all by selling top-secret information to the pirates."

But while she said that she knew it wasn't really the same. And he knew it, too. She wasn't very good at finding appropriate metaphors. Besides, her family was neither famous nor rich.

Finn sighed. "All I wanted to say is that things aren't usually as black and white as all that."

"You're finding very convoluted ways of saying it."

He sighed. "I'm sorry. I'm not very good at this."

"Is that why you've been grumpy?"

He shrugged and said nothing for a while.

Tina stared at the blinking lights on the controls. They were blue lights and blue lights were good.

Tina was about to push off to get back to her many tasks when Finn motioned for her to stay.

"I'm busy."

"It's important you understand what I'm going to say."

Now he was going to talk, after months in space?

He continued, "I just want to let you know that there are many other interests in this particular case."

"What is that supposed to mean?"

"The information we're delivering to the Assembly. Other people would love to have it."

"I'm sure that's never entered my mind." She made sure to say that as sarcastically as possible.

"No, you don't understand. Bluntly speaking: when your husband sold his material to the pirates, you think no one else would have been interested in it?"

He now met Tina's eyes and a deep chill went through her.

Olympus Pharmaceuticals was one of the most powerful companies in human settled space. They were very much into genetic modification, all in the name of medicine.

Who knew what levels of interest Dexter was trying to fend off when he went to that meeting where he passed samples of particles to people outside Project Charon? People who had later gone to the pirates, or turned out to be pirates, or *become* pirates because of their contact with the interdimensional particles?

Of course a pharmaceutical company would have been interested, too, because of the endless medicinal potential of this material.

Take this pill and you will live for a long time and become very smart, but oh, you'll also end up looking like a warty toad.

But it was never like that, was it? Scientists would research, work at and take apart the material until they had separated its desired components from the undesirable ones.

The stage of the process she had witnessed was the very beginning, and the Federacy was going: whoa, we have this stuff coming out of another universe, it looks like it's dangerous. Everyone keep their hands off it.

And that situation never lasted because people didn't stick to those rules. The Federacy hadn't done a particularly good job of protecting the secret that an interdimensional rift existed. It hadn't done well in managing the rift material. They had downplayed the danger and attempted to stick the discovery away in some dusty research file.

Except the rumour had already gotten out.

People had become frustrated at the Project's management of the data, not just the ones who wanted it kept away from other people, but those who advocated for making the dust available for research as well.

And so Dexter had passed it to other parties. His motive might have been money, but she thought that unlikely. Dexter was a lot of things, but greedy for cash wasn't one of them. Greedy for power, now that was another matter. He might have been authorised to hand it out by the high command. The military might have realised they were out of their depth and might have been looking for a partner. They might have wanted to keep the meeting secret so as not to invite the naysayers.

Whatever. From that meeting, it ended up with the pirates.

Olympus Pharmaceuticals had missed out on it. They might not have been invited to the initial meeting with Dexter, or might have been there but made too many demands or bid too low.

Maybe Olympus Pharmaceuticals had sent Finn to find her, under the guise of being employed as a ship engineer, and he was just here to keep an eye on her so she arrived at Olympus safely. So the company could then exert pressure on her to hand over her data.

She felt cold. She had trusted him, and even liked him, but clearly trust was a fragile thing.

He was still looking at her.

She nodded to indicate that she understood. "So your family has sent you to chaperone us?"

"No, I swear they don't know about us, about me being here."

"But?" There clearly was a but.

"I'm not so sure anymore that it's good idea to take your knowledge to Olympus."

"What? You were all for it. The Federacy Assembly seems the logical place to take it. Besides, I don't know that we have anything they don't already know."

"It's about this."

He moved the stand with his reader closer so that she could see the screen. It displayed a very unexciting document from the Space Settlers' Health Commission. Tina blinked at it, since the article was a giant wall of text.

"Read it," Finn said.

Tina had to make an effort to concentrate. Fuzziness on the brain was a well-known after-effect of the jump.

The headline read:

Notification of reward money worth two million credits

Leading to a treatment or vaccine to stop the spread of what has become popularly known as "pirate disease", the malformation of skin and extremities, followed by malformation of internal structures, followed by de-humanisation of the body.

Tina looked up. "They're looking for a cure. I could use two million credits."

"Yes. So could many people. What do you think they'll do for it?"

"When was this posted?"

"A month ago. If scientists find this cure, those scientists will be employed by a company, most likely one who helped fund the reward."

"Your family?"

He shrugged, looking unhappy. "I don't know. I can't tell from this document. I can't really contact them and ask. It's the sort of thing you talk about in private functions, not through transmitted speech, which is recorded and can be traced. The company who finds this cure will screw the Federacy out of as much money as possible by making their *cure* expensive. The pirates will want to get their hands on it just so they can destroy it, because they like the mutations and the strength they gain from them. A cure wouldn't be just a cure, but a way to make a lot of money over the backs of a lot of desperate people."

"But I'm not the solution and I don't have the solution."

"Yet. You have to admit you have a couple of very valuable pieces."

She did. Both she and Rex were resistant, especially Rex. She had discovered the three-strand DNA mutations, and she had data from the original material that could teach scientists how it had developed and how it would develop in the future. And she had the cactuses that already developed along a trajectory, and were still doing so. They were changing every day.

Also, she had a paper about to be published on the subject that—damn—had already drawn the eyes of the entire scientific community. Should she stop its publication? Was that even possible?

"Why do you think we shouldn't go to the Assembly? In a case like this, it seems the perfect place to go. They're independent."

"Because the Federacy Assembly don't have a research arm, so they'll pass it on to a company and that company is interested in only one thing: making money. Trust me, I might not know that much about pirates, but I know that world. They will sell their own children to the highest bidders. It's all about money."

"What would you like me to do then? Hand it to your family's company?"

"Look, I understand that you're suspicious of me. I would be, too, if I were in your shoes."

"But you're not."

"Whatever you think, I'm here for one thing: to make sure the information doesn't fall into the wrong hands, and that you and Rex don't end up paying for it with your freedom or your lives."

"So? You want me to hand it to your family so that they can do the right thing?"

"You're not listening to me."

"You're not telling me anything new. What do you want me to do?"

"We should do the science ourselves."

"Just the two of us?" Develop the cure and get two million credits.

"We can employ people."

Her own company, with her own employees and her own agenda. Tina kind of liked that idea. But the thought that she could take on the big pharmaceutical industries was ridiculous. Not only that, she doubted two million credits was enough to fund that sort of operation. No, it was a reward designed for people like herself to come forward.

Still, she liked the thought of going back into research. In her mind, she was already building a new lab over the burnt-out ruins of her shop in Gandama. She could be a catalyst for the development that had been planned for the region, but that never happened.

"I have to think about that for a bit." This was not at all what she'd expected to hear. "In the more immediate future, we'll still be visiting Aurora. I presume you anticipate some competition or bounty hunters to turn up there."

"Yes. And it's now too late to do anything about it."

"You said nothing when it was not too late."

"I did say something."

"Nothing specific. Just vague stories about people not liking your family. I can't do anything with vague stories. If I'd known this before..." She spread her hands, because what did she really know that she hadn't known before? That people were after what she knew? That she was wanted by certain authorities, including for damaging station structures at Kelso Station? "I'd probably still have decided to come here over going to Beta."

"There you go. No point me mentioning anything. You're as stubborn as my mother."

Tina snorted. Men! "From someone who organises pissing contests in the cargo hold, I'll take that as a compliment."

CHAPTER FIVE

WAS Tina right to have trusted him? She didn't know anymore.

It was all very well to make self-righteous judgements about commercial companies and the interests of pirates, but one thing Finn was right about: there was a lot of interest in the alien dust, and no clear "right" thing to do with it.

But she wasn't ready to have that discussion now. She'd make up her mind once the ship was refuelled and resupplied.

There was more work to be done. Tina was running out of space for the cactuses in the cabin behind the control room. Rasa had made a cage for the geese and the cactuses sat against the wall behind it. Because this section was in zero-g, it was sufficient to simply tie the pots to the wall. They had already installed some lights. She had to lop off a couple of extra fronds, because they were too close to the cage. Tina measured the length of a goose's neck and made sure the cactuses stayed at least that distance from the cage.

When the time came to move the geese, Rasa would wrap them in a cloth bag and tie up their wings so they didn't go flapping about the cage and injure themselves or spread feather fluff through the air.

But as she had already predicted, she ran out of space. There was no room elsewhere in the four cabins, so the remaining cactuses would have to go into the cold and dark cargo hold, with the hope that their stay would be short enough to allow them to survive. She did manage to find one light to provide warmth, but she doubted that was enough, and they were running out of time because so much else needed to be moved.

Coming back into the cabins in the main body of the craft, she met Rasa carrying a bewildered goose under her arm. As they had proposed, the bird's wings were already tied up, because fluff of feather in zero-g really messed with the air filters.

"That's the last one," Rasa said cheerfully.

The bird didn't look impressed.

Rasa went into the cabin that held the cage. She opened the door and pushed the goose in. It honked and flapped about with its feet without finding purchase. Rasa pulled the bird back up straight. The cloth bag attached to a hook on the inside top of the cage. A second hook attached to the bottom of the cage, and the goose could "sit" on a beam that stretched across the cage. The other birds were already in their positions. And one of them had already discovered the cactuses, snaking its neck out of the cage to try to reach the plants. By the look of things, it would cover the distance, too, especially if the plants moved during ship manoeuvres.

"No, no, don't do that!"

Tina pushed herself into the room, checked that the pots were properly secured to the wall, and tied them down with another strap.

Rasa shut the door to the cage.

But things tended to jiggle in this part of the craft, and because there was no particular direction for them to jiggle in, they jiggled in all directions. That was bad, because they came loose all the time. This was why Tina had wanted to cannibalise some locking mechanisms from the cargo door airlock.

Now they needed to remember to check inside the cabin before opening the door fully. Hopefully the bags to hold their wings made the spread of feathers less, because that first time the geese got loose in the cabin during flight was a nightmare. Especially since the panicked geese kept flying into everything and bouncing off the walls.

All right, so that was done.

Now for the last comfortable shower until they docked at the station and would have gravity again.

Coming down into the gym and greenhouse, she realised that someone was already in the shower cabin.

Was it time for Rex to use it already?

She checked. It was.

Despite not needing assistance to take the harness off and clean the attachment points every day, they'd learned during the trip that it was still a good idea to let other people assist Rex in checking the harness' attachment points. He couldn't see them properly himself, and a closed-environment atmosphere was a perfect breeding ground for infections.

So she had taught Finn to help Rex, and later Rasa as well, when observing the level of care with which the girl groomed and washed her geese.

In fact, Rasa had taken to the task quite well.

She and Rex swapped jobs, because Rex would sometimes catch and brush the geese, collecting downy feathers in a bag so that they didn't go floating about the habitat.

But when Tina came into the gym, Rasa quickly pulled the door to the cubicle shut.

That was strange.

Why would she...?

Damn.

Rex had turned sixteen since leaving Kelso. He might not be a normal teenage boy, but he was definitely a teenage boy, with interests that aligned with teenage boys.

She stared at the closed door, listening for... she didn't know what. But the only thing she could hear was the hiss of humid air out of the nozzles, and the sound of the pump that circulated the water vapour.

Should she knock and demand the door be left open, like usual? Or should she treat him as the adult he claimed to be and give him privacy?

But was she ready for that particular kind of privacy?

Tina went to the spot where the cactuses no longer stood, picking up a few prickly fronds, while listening for sounds from the bathroom.

She didn't hear anything unusual, other than the hiss of the humid air out of the nozzles, and occasional talking. Surely she was imagining things.

While she waited, she collected the last tomatoes, pulled out the plants and put them in the recycler, and drifted up to the storage room in the main part of the ship where she placed them with the other food supplies.

When she passed through the cabin, Finn was sitting at the controls of the ship, staring into the distance.

"Going well?" he asked her.

"Almost done," she said. "We'll be able to fold everything up after dinner."

She thought about saying more, or even asking him for

advice, but what did he know about teenage boys? More often than not, he acted like one himself.

Tina went back down into the gym, at which time Rex and Rasa came out talking about something that they had to fix.

Tina met Rex's eyes. His expression was open and honest and, if she was looking for a sign of guilt, she saw none.

Damn.

He had only just turned sixteen. That was no age to…

She'd been sixteen.

And of course she lived on a farm with lots of wide fields. She doubted her parents ever knew what went on in the copse of trees by the dry creek bed. None of it had done any harm to her, even if the boy later turned out to be a dick who went on to serially date almost every girl in the senior class at school.

In this ship, there was, of course, a way to find out what happened at any time in every room. The ship recorded everything on the security cameras for safety reasons. She bet Rex didn't know this. If she wanted to know what was going on in the bathroom, all she needed to do was play back the recording.

She thought about it, hesitated when she came to the cabin, and then decided it was a cowardly thing to do. She would have to have the talk with Rex at some point very soon. It was something she had never envisaged doing, because she had never thought that any girl would be interested in him in his state.

In a way, it was weirdly satisfactory. Her son had gone from being a cripple in a clunky harness to becoming a normal teenage boy.

CHAPTER SIX

"WOW LOOK AT THAT. It's huge," Rex said.

He sat in the seat behind Tina, now strapped in, because the habitat was stowed away, folded against the body of the ship, and they were about to arrive on Aurora Station. He was looking at the screen, where the magnificent structure of Aurora Space Station was displayed.

It was much bigger than Kelso. Kelso had grown a lot in Tina's absence, but this thing was huge.

The main body of the station consisted of a number of rings fixed on top of each other. Many structures floated off the sides and ends of the rings, making the whole structure look like a giant spider.

Ships could dock on both sides of the station, through a central docking system like the one at Kelso. The public and passenger access was on this side, the supply docks on the other.

A voice from Station Control sounded in Tina's ear. "Identify yourself to be placed in the docking queue." It was a female voice, likely automated, that sounded, to her mind, too normal for a space station in pirate hands.

Tina gave the station the ship's identification number, hoping that Kelso hadn't put through the warning about them having left illegally without paying some of their debts.

As far as Tina had heard, the pirates had also occupied Kelso, which meant that all the authorities would probably be in too much disarray to keep track of unpaid docking fees.

Or so Tina hoped.

The voice didn't raise any trouble. It gave Tina coordinates and an estimated time for the docking procedure to begin.

She turned around to the others. "It sounds quite normal. They're just giving me the procedures. Nothing about us should catch their attention. I've put us in as a commercial vessel."

There was a lot of traffic, which was a good sign, even if it remained to be seen what sort of commercial services the station would still provide to visiting ships.

Rex said from the front passenger bench, "Is anyone else getting the station's newsfeed?"

"Sorry, too busy to check," Tina said. "Have a look to see if we've missed anything important."

"It says the Federacy has taken back Kelso, and there's been fighting around Peris City."

"Federacy against pirates?"

"It doesn't say. I think so."

"Whereabouts?"

"There's no more information."

Tina thought of her shop, already burned. Pirates already lived in desert caves. What was the chance that this fighting was near Gandama? "Does it say anything important about Aurora?"

Rex scrolled through the feed, the glow from the screen lighting his face. He read, "Aurora Station Director Zia Partlow says that she regrets the existence of the wait, and they are working on resolving the situation—"

"Wait for what?" Tina asked.

"It says here that there are wait times for most station services. Hang on, here's another one." He paused before continuing, "Director Partlow also stresses that people should stay calm on the subject of absent friends or family members. She insists, 'We are working with the new station ownership to resolve the issue.' A spokesperson from the protest groups responded that the population of Aurora had given her a lot of time already and patience was running out."

Tina had no idea what all this was about and definitely didn't like the sound of it but had no intention of becoming involved.

Then she saw the expression on Finn's face.

"What's wrong?"

"I told you we shouldn't come here."

"Why not? I don't see anything to worry about."

"There is everything to worry about. Zia Partlow."

"Do you know her?"

"She is from the Partlow family, who owns Partlow Industries."

That rang a bell with Tina. "Don't they make space suits?"

"Yes, and much more, including pharmaceuticals."

Now that made a lot more sense, considering his earlier words. "So they're a competitor of yours."

The operator's voice blared in her ear, and, as Finn had predicted, it now asked for the names of the crew and passengers of the ship.

Tina gave them their false names. She hoped that the

name Freeman was common enough that no one would suspect Rex of being her son, and she also hoped that Rasa's name would not have any warnings against it, because there were plenty of red flags there, too. For one, Rasa had an ID chip implanted which had to mean she came from a well-off background. A story was waiting to come out about Rasa's family, and Tina hoped it didn't do so at an inconvenient time.

The station's auto-vetting system had no issues with Louise Metvier, David Metz, Rex Freeman or Rasa Vichenko.

Once she'd supplied the names and reason for visiting—for a meeting with a scientific buyer—the station allowed them into the arrivals queue, where station control would take over the operations of the ship so it would dock safely and in the allocated slot.

Rex looked on in amazement. Like this, he was still very much a little boy, even though he could break bones with the grip of his new metal hands. Even if Tina caught him glancing sideways at Rasa, lifting the corner of his mouth.

"There are so many ships here," he said.

That was hopefully their protection. Aurora was such a big place, it would be easy to go unnoticed as just another visiting commercial ship. A station like this needed a constant stream of commercial vessels to survive. Whoever sat in the control room wasn't going to make much difference to that type of traffic.

She hoped.

Tina considered her shopping list. They would need fuel and food, some clothes for Rasa, food for the geese, and parts for the ship, including a fix for the inverter.

How long would that take? How easy would it be to find Rex's friend, who might be enticed to help them for little cost? How much risk was there, when they only needed to buy a few things and get out again? Especially when they left Finn on board the ship.

The ship connected with the station's docking structure and gravity returned with a lurch. A few items dislodged in one of the cabins. A loud honking came from the cabin that held the geese.

"I better go and check them," Rasa said. She went into the back of the ship while the docking mechanism trundled further along the arm, increasing the gravity.

Tina could hear the sound of a door rolling aside, and then a cry from Rasa.

The next moment, three geese flew through the cabin, narrowly missing Rex.

"Get those bloody birds out of here!" Tina called out.

One flew on top of the headrest of the seat next to her. Finn sat here. He ducked out of the way of the goose's flapping wings.

Rasa came up from behind with the cloth bag, and trapped the animal. This resulted in much squawking and distribution of fluff.

"It's always the same one that's naughty," Rasa said, while carrying the protesting goose back to the cabin. The other two followed meekly.

But in the cabin with the geese, the devastation was much greater than expected. Not only had the geese escaped from the bags that tied their wings together, and from the cage, but they'd been getting into the cactuses. Entire plants had been ripped from the wall and out of their pots.

"Oh, I'm so sorry," Rasa said. "I don't understand why they like these plants. They normally only like seeds. I'll help you clean it up."

It was a while until the doors could be opened, so Tina

collected the vacuum cleaner and cleaned up the mess made by the geese. They had pulled a couple of plants right out of their pots. The fronds carried bite marks. All the little seed buds had been bitten off. She had intended to grow those seeds, even if only to have something to do on the way to Olympus. Those geese were really very troublesome.

They protested loudly while Tina and Rasa were cleaning, honking at the vacuum cleaner as she dragged it past their cage.

"I am really sorry," Rasa said when they were done. "I try really hard to lock them up but they always escape."

"Just... let's try to find some parts to fix that lock." Tina let out a sigh. Rasa did try hard; she knew that. There was no point saying that geese weren't ideal space passengers, because everyone knew that, too. The geese were the only things Rasa owned, and they had to come wherever Rasa went.

"I'll get some parts. Trade them for eggs."

"It's all right. I'll put it on the account."

Tina was about to go back to the cabin, hesitated at the door, but then she decided to plunge in. It might be easier to speak to Rasa than to Rex.

"You like Rex?" she asked.

Rasa nodded. "He's nice." But she didn't meet Tina's eyes. Her cheeks coloured.

That was just as Tina feared.

"If there is... anything you want to talk about, I'm always here."

"No. There is nothing." And after a short and uncomfortable silence, Rasa continued, "I better bring the tub of grain in here."

And before Tina could say anything else, anything even more awkward, she was gone.

This talking-to-teenager thing was not going very well.

CHAPTER SEVEN

TINA RETURNED TO THE CABIN, her cheeks glowing. She wasn't sure what to think. Rex was still her baby and she didn't want to lose him yet. But it was amazing that she even had thoughts about what he might do to girls in locked shower cubicles.

The movement of the ship stopped and a message came from the station that the docking tube was about to be connected.

"Do you see those ships over there?" Finn asked. He pointed an outside camera at a section of the docking rig where a number of ships were moored. They were ugly things, dark and square, the surface weathering consistent with having spent considerable time in deep space.

"I presume those are pirate ships?" Tina asked.

"They're certainly not Federacy warships," Finn said.

"Have you actually been here before?"

"I haven't. The warships don't come to Aurora. It's a fully civilian station, and they have no military supply base here."

"That never stopped them coming before." And she meant before he joined the Force.

"Not if there is a reason, no. But they say that officially the risk of compromise is too high. In a civilian station it's too easy for someone to infiltrate a large population and sabotage ship supplies."

The sounds outside the hull were now gentler: soft hums and beeps and hissing, as the entry tube connected.

"Well, it seems we'll find out what's going on here," Tina said. "I'm trying to keep our time here as short as possible, and I'm going to order supplies as soon as they let us off."

Tina went to the sleeping cabin she'd shared with Rasa over the past few days. During flight, these cabins were weightless, but now the ship had been attached to the station, she could walk into them again. Of course, stuff was on the floor. A blanket lay weirdly draped over a chair and a dry soap dispenser had landed on the bottom bunk when gravity returned to the ship. For some reason, you always ended up forgetting to secure something.

The geese in the cabin across the passage were making a racket.

Tina changed into what she hoped were inconspicuous clothes: a ship overall and sturdy workboots.

When she came out of the cabin, Rex stood at the end of the short hallway.

"Can I come?"

"I won't be very long."

"I don't mind."

"Have you heard from your friend yet?"

"Not yet."

Tina looked from Finn to Rasa.

"I'm not coming," Finn said.

Rasa shook her head.

"All right. Let's go quickly."

Tina didn't like leaving the two of them on board the ship. Finn didn't like the geese, and Rasa was sure to let them out. It was not a happy combination.

Tina opened first the inner and then the outer door, letting in a waft of humid air.

Rex pulled a face.

"This place stinks," he said.

It did. The air was slightly too warm and smelled of cooking—reminding Tina of her time on board the large vessels—and wet laundry that had been sitting in a basket for too long.

That was probably not a good sign for the health of the station. But the corridor outside the docking tube looked orderly enough, so Tina and Rex ventured into the station.

First they walked along a passage with docking tubes on both sides. Almost all of them were in use. The whole area was a hive of the usual type of activity: people walking in and out of ships, maintenance crews moving about, and people in station overalls wheeling trolleys with small deliveries.

They walked past larger docking tubes where people waited to be allowed on board. At other tubes, dockworkers in station overalls were unloading small parcels from ships. People met each other in meeting rooms. A woman was giving a presentation in a room with glass walls. A dozen or so people sat listening and watching the screen behind her, which displayed some kind of electronic device. Something she was selling, Tina assumed.

So far, the station appeared very businesslike, and not at all how she had imagined a pirate-run station to be. Perhaps this was why they didn't like to be called pirates.

Tina and Rex followed the signs that pointed to the port authority.

In the busy office, they completed the formalities in relation to their identification and the ship and their preferred departure date. Tina said "as soon as possible" but she noticed how none of the dates she spotted on the woman's screen were closer than a week. The woman then asked details about the ship, including the number of passengers it was licensed to take.

Tina asked her about getting supplies, but was informed that she would need to go into the station's commercial sector, where she could find the Ship Supply office. So they went in search of that through a well-signposted maze of passages.

The station bore all the signs of a well-organised operation. This would not be so hard after all.

"I don't understand why Finn is so scared," Tina said.

"Yeah. Jens told me the place was in chaos. This is a lot better than Kelso Station."

But then they turned a corner, where the sounds of agitated voices reached them. In the passage ahead was a kind of roadblock, a metal grate that stretched from wall to wall and up to the ceiling.

Two guards stood on the other side, with their backs to Tina and Rex, holding back a crowd of people. The air coming out of the passage was warm and smelled rank with grime and unclean people.

Someone in the group spotted Tina and Rex.

A man shouted.

"What are they saying?" Rex asked.

"I have no idea. It sounds like Sinolese to me."

"And you don't even understand Sinolese?"

"Smartarse."

Rex grinned, but Tina felt uneasy.

These people were civilians. They didn't sound happy.

Why the metal grate and the guards? To keep the clean docks separate from the unwashed rest of the station?

The guards turned around and waited until Tina and Rex came to them.

"I'm in search of the Ship Supply office," Tina said. "We're probably lost."

"No, this is the right way. It's in the hall just around the corner."

Through there? "Can we visit it?"

"If you have valid ID."

Tina dug in her pocket for Louisa Metvier's ID.

The guards took it, displaying no emotion on their faces. They said nothing about danger, or even about how to get through this mass of people.

One man put the card in a really old scanner—didn't they have modern equipment? Even the one she had in the ship was more recent.

All these transactions were conducted through the bars of the grate.

For a brief moment, Tina had a vision of these men taking off with her ID. They would be helpless.

"Your reason for your visit to Aurora?" one man asked.

"I'm in need of ship supplies," Tina said. "I have some business contacts on the station that I need to visit."

"You're going to have to join the queue for ship supplies," one of the men said.

"How long?"

"If you're lucky, two weeks."

Two weeks? Two weeks for a process that shouldn't take more than half a day?

But Tina didn't say anything, because people at the front of the crowd were listening.

Further back, people stood on their toes to catch a glimpse of her and Rex.

"What are all these people doing here?"

The guard laughed. "Wherever have you come from?"

"Kelso."

"Where is that?" He and his mate laughed again.

That was a very strange and unprofessional reaction. Both men wore shirts with the station authority's logo, but the trousers were non-standard and worn. Also, she didn't believe those were official-issue stunners that they carried on their belts.

Not real guards at all. Huh.

"These people are waiting for available flights off the station, but passenger places are in short supply. You can make quite a bit by taking a few passengers when you leave."

"I think we're OK. We're quite full already."

"All right. Suit yourself.

He undid the lock at the top and bottom of the grate, and opened the door.

The people started shouting louder. The guard shouted for them to move aside, but the reaction was unconvincing.

"I'll go first," Rex said.

The people shrank back from Rex, staring up at his metal body. Tina followed close behind, feeling small.

A couple of people tried asking her questions.

Tina didn't understand their language, but then a woman said, "How much?"

Tina looked at her. How much what? The woman was skinny with pleading dark eyes.

"You have a ship, right?" She had a young child with her, a skinny thing with large eyes and a smudge on his forehead.

"Are you all waiting to be taken off the station?"

Rex had stopped, and more people crowded around them.

"Keep moving, keep moving!" The guards yelled over the heads of the crowd. "Keep moving. We don't want any trouble. We got to keep them quiet."

"I'm sorry," Tina said to the woman, even if she didn't know what to be sorry for.

She left the woman and followed Rex through the crowd, trying to ignore further questions. She had already taken Rasa on board. She was doing her bit for humanity, right?

Then the crowd thinned out, and she caught up with Rex.

"Mum, did you see that ancient scanner they were using?" Rex said in a low voice.

"Shhh."

"And then that gate. I bet I could rip that out of the wall if I wanted." He flexed his metal hands. Rex had been doing a lot of exercises with his new harness during the journey from Kelso. He had become quite handy with it.

"Shhh," Tina said again. "I have no idea who's listening, but someone is bound to keep an eye on us. I didn't like those guards at all."

CHAPTER EIGHT

AT THE END of the passage, Tina and Rex came to a spacious atrium area that would have been sleek and modern if it hadn't been crammed with people and noise.

The air was so hazy that the far end of the space—large enough to show the curvature of the floor—disappeared into a bluish mist.

They really had a problem with dust and clean air here. This couldn't be sustainable or healthy for the station. Everywhere Tina looked, crowds and lines of people waited to enter offices.

A long line of people accompanied by travel bags stretched across the hall. Some people had sat down, and others were even asleep with her heads on their luggage. Men looked unshaven, women were dishevelled, children whined.

How many days had they been waiting here?

"Where do all these people come from?" Tina asked, not that she expected Rex to know the answer.

"The news says there has been conflict at the outstations," Rex said. His new harness gave him access to all the online information at the touch of a finger. He'd been much delighted with the screen that folded out from his arm that provided him with information, including the news, but also diagnostics on electronics he was working on.

"Which are these outstations?" Tina asked.

He read off the screen. "A number of mining stations that supply Aurora Station. Apparently some of them have become unstable, and the inhabitants have fled while the Pirates and the Federacy Force are fighting over who owns them."

And that would mean a great number of people had streamed into the station, and now the station might be over capacity, which explained the humid foul tang of the air.

Then he added, "Oh, and it says here the habitat of Beta Station is about to collapse."

"Just as well we didn't go there, then."

Tina and Rex found the Ship Supply office on the second floor gallery of the large hall. The queue stretched out the door.

Tina joined it bravely, and soon a number of people filed behind her. But the same people were still at the front. If they were going to wait here, they would still be waiting tomorrow morning.

There was a ticketing system in place, but no one appeared to be using it. Tina asked about it.

"Sure, you can get a number and come back later to see how far it's gone down the line," a woman who was also waiting said. "But everyone knows your turn comes up much more quickly when you stay here."

"And how long would that be?"

"A few days."

A few days sounded better than two weeks. Maybe they

could manage a few days. If waiting here could cut the time from two weeks to a few days, then it might be wise to stay.

A good number of children waited in the line, some sitting patiently on their bags. A few others were talking to each other.

A teenage boy came in, and spoke to a younger boy who was waiting. The boy hopped off the suitcase and scampered out the door while the older one took the position.

That was how other people managed it: they took turns.

They could manage that, too, if they all took turns waiting here.

Tina and Rex waited a bit longer, because Tina wanted to see what would be required of them once their turn came up. She asked some people.

A man had been waiting for two days. He said it would be his turn in another two or three days. He also said supplies were expensive, but he'd heard they were delivered promptly.

A woman said she'd been through the system a few times. Sometimes the supply office made everyone wait and nothing happened for days and all of a sudden they approved and supplied every ship and cleared everyone out of the docks fast. She had even heard that, in extreme cases, no one was charged for the supplies.

That seemed a bit of a wishful thinking folk tale, but someone else chimed in that he had heard that, too. But you never knew when it would happen.

"It throws my entire schedule into disarray, I tell you, to be told to leave when I haven't finished business yet." The man was holding commercial papers. He had to be a private courier. "These days I avoid coming here if I can."

It seemed a great source of frustration that people couldn't get supplies quickly because they wanted to leave, and she also heard that if you had a passenger ship, the delivery of supplies might be conditioned on the agreement to take as many passengers as your ship would take off the station.

Which was, of course, why they had asked about the ship's capacity.

If that happened, did they have any choice in passengers?

Tina asked around, but people gave different answers. It seemed to depend on who handled your case.

The people on the other side of the counter were a mixture of men and women, young and old. None of them looked fairer or more bribable than any other. Were you meant to bribe them? If so, they were stuck here.

Maybe bribes could be bought according to the number of passengers you took off the station. If so, they were still stuck. The ship was licensed to take eight, but it had been crowded enough with four.

She said to Rex, "I think I'd like to talk to a local. You said something about meeting your friend?"

"Jens?"

"Yes. Can you get in contact with him?"

"I could…"

"But?"

"It's kind of strange. You were never interested in any of my friends before."

"We were never here to meet them."

"All right."

He shrugged and a kind of uneasy silence passed. Tina wanted to ask "Well, why don't you contact him?" but she remembered a particularly embarrassing occasion when her father had insisted on coming with her to meet some boys from her school, because "it's important to see the people you hang out with." It was because she was fourteen, and because her friend was a boy, like most of her friends. They talked to each other about getting parts to build things, and then building those things. Nothing was going on between her and those boys, and having her father there was super awkward, because of the way they spoke to each other, which included a lot of swearing.

So she told Rex, "I might go for a walk while you do this, to see if I can find out anything useful. If you don't mind staying here, that is."

Rex said he didn't.

So Tina left him in the queue. She wasn't going to be the embarrassing parent.

From the first floor gallery, she could see over the railing onto the ground floor of the atrium. Underneath the first floor gallery on the opposite side were some shops. Maybe she'd be able to buy some supplies there.

But the shops were low on stock, and what they had was hideously expensive, even more so if you couldn't show proof of residency. And at the shops that sold major survival items, like food, the queues were out the door.

There were some decent second-hand clothing shops, where Tina bought a few basic things for Rasa: two pairs of plain ship overalls, some shirts and a stack of socks.

Standing in a shop looking at overpriced packets of dried ship biscuits, Tina overheard two women complain. Most people on Aurora spoke a Transigian dialect of Sinolese that Tina found hard to understand, but these two had to be from either Olympus or her home world of Tirkala.

"I managed to get a whole crate of milk powder rations," one of the women was saying.

"A whole crate? Where did you get that?"

"Oh, my brother has connections."

"Must be really good connections. Wonder how much you paid?"

"It's not about that. I went to exchange some packets for different items, but they wouldn't let me into the market hall without registering as a merchant."

The other woman snorted. "And here was I, thinking that these so-called pirates didn't want to meddle with our business. Isn't that what the creep said? What his name again?"

"Artan. Piece of filth."

"You said it. No, they didn't want to have rules. But they were lying. They didn't want *our* rules. Nothing wrong with *their* rules."

The women's discussion encapsulated, in a nutshell, the feeling that Tina had formed so far about pirate-occupied space. It was unregulated chaos into which someone had attempted to insert some belated rules to make sure the station didn't destroy itself.

It was also the first time she'd heard any of the pirates named. Artan. She wondered what was known about him.

She walked through the corridors of the commercial section, making sure to record as she went so she could play it back to Finn, who might be persuaded to leave the ship. If this went on too long, he would probably need to leave the ship anyway, because they would be allocated to an area where residence on the ships was restricted.

The commercial section of Aurora Station was much busier than that at Kelso.

But during her walk, she spotted no people who were obvious pirates. In fact, there were no figures of authority at all, no one to lead the crowds into orderly paths. No one to tell anyone what was going on.

A news screen at the ground floor in the atrium displayed

looping video clips of a promotional type. A space fleet, a mass of cheering people. The sound from the clip was drowned out by the ambient noise in the hall.

It could be news. It could be propaganda. It could be advertising for some kind of entertainment, for all she knew.

A lot of beggars sat on the corners. As soon as you stopped, someone came up to you asking you for something, not usually money, because they had plenty of that, but food or a lift off the station. Most of these scruffy people looked like they had been there for a long time.

The shops were very busy, too, and, as far as she could tell, none of them carried ship supplies. You could buy fresh fruit and vegetables, but those were from the farms on the station. She needed vacuum-packed food that would keep for a number of months. Those packages were only sold at the Ship Supply office.

So she returned to Rex, finding that he had moved only a little bit up the queue.

"I heard from Jens," he said. "He's still here and happy to see us."

"You know what? We'll take the number. We can always come back later and resume waiting." She wasn't keen to leave anyone here in this soulless queue.

It was really going to take two weeks, wasn't it? Two weeks during which they always had to have one person inside this damn queue. And then to hope that by the time they got to the front, she had all the documentation and they would accept her credit.

There had to be a different way.

CHAPTER NINE

BUT REX DIDN'T WANT to leave his position.

Tina told him to come back with her, but he said, "No mum, it's exactly like at Gandama. They want you to line up, and if you haven't waited then they won't give you whatever it is that you want. They'll penalise you for not doing as they say, like when we tried to get them to build a water tank."

Yes, Tina remembered that well. It had been hard enough to get all the people at Dickson's Creek to put their signature to it, and then the officials did everything they could to say that they hadn't followed the correct procedures. Of course, Dickson's Creek still had no tank. "You might have a point there."

Rex smiled. He had become so much more mature recently.

"But how are we going to go about meeting Jens?"

"I'll ask him and let him suggest how to meet him."

"We can't ask Finn to stand here."

"I'm not sure why not," Rex said. "I know he doesn't want to, but I don't see any evidence of violence."

"The place is chaotic. Nothing more dramatic than Kelso. The pirates seem to rule by absence."

"Has Finn ever said to you why he doesn't want to come here?"

"Nothing more than the story you've already heard. That his family has an issue with some people here. Because the pharmaceutical world is such a violent place."

Rex chuckled. "I know, right?"

"I'm sure we're happy not to know about plenty in his world, and this station is big enough to harbour all kinds of unsavoury people, but they don't have to *know* he's here. He's even got the fake identity to match."

"Yes, we'll tell him he needs to take his turn."

"I'm more concerned about Rasa."

He nodded, concern on his face.

"Do you know whether she has a history with this station?" Rasa had been very evasive about her past, but maybe she had told Rex more about it.

"She's never been here."

"I'm afraid that her tattoo has a meaning in terms of her ownership by a pimp or something. Do you know anything about it?"

"I don't think it means anything like that. Anyway, she's never been to Aurora, so she should be safe from that kind of thing."

"Some of these criminal rings are widely spread." Yet Tina hadn't been able to find images of the tattoo, so it wasn't one of the bigger gangs.

They decided Rex would stay for the time being.

When Tina returned to the ship alone, Rasa was very concerned where Rex was.

Tina explained about the queues and that it seemed better

to leave him there, because that seemed to be the way people got supplies and everybody else was doing this as well. They would have to take turns.

"But how long is that going to take?" Finn said. He seemed still anxious.

"We can only wait. We need the supplies, and we can't go without them, so we don't have an option."

"I said we shouldn't have come here," Finn said.

"I went for a walk into the station, and I didn't see anything that worried me. Mostly just a lot of people hanging around waiting. I didn't see any pirates or any violence or signs of past violence. I also heard that there is severe trouble at Beta Station."

Finn gave her a dark look. "You're only saying that to spite me."

"No, I am not. It's in the news. You can look it up. You can go into the station yourself and see how crowded the place is. The guards at the gate also said that it was likely that people wanted us to take some refugees off the station in return for getting our supplies."

"I told you we'd be overrun."

"It doesn't look like overrunning to me. They were waiting, and apparently you can buy favours by taking passengers."

"They're only doing that to create trouble in our crews, or to get their most troublesome people off the station."

"It doesn't look that way to me. It looks like the station is genuinely in trouble and overcrowded, and a lot of these people genuinely have nowhere else to go."

At this, Rasa nodded. "Some of the stations are like that. They just allow the people to come in, and then they use them as hostages."

"But why would they do that? It destabilises the station."

"To create an emergency so they get money," was Finn's dark reply.

"But they already get money," Tina said. Authorities were always complaining about how much they needed to pay for standardised docking facilities at stations.

"It's often not enough, and payment is usually late," Finn said. "But create an emergency and something is done quickly. Letting a lot of people die on your watch looks messy and is terrible for PR."

"But the station is in pirate hands," Tina said.

"I promise you: the Partlow family are a lot of things, but pirates, they are not. They look out only for themselves. They'll do anything to get money."

"Why would Federacy send them money, though? If they're under pirate rule, they're more likely to send troops."

Finn met her eyes and in them, she saw that he knew she was right. "All the more reason to get out of here fast."

He held his hands clasped on his knees. "While we're talking about this, there is one other thing you need to know. I don't know how important it's going to be, but you seem to have a habit of questioning everything I say. For one, it might convince you I know what I'm talking about. It's about the station director at Aurora, Zia Partlow. For a brief period in my stupid youth, she used to be my wife."

"You were married?"

"It was the biggest disaster of my life. I did what my family wanted. It was supposed to bring together two dynasties and create a bond. From day one my family-in-law belittled, insulted and outright threatened me. My new wife originally tried to shelter me from it, but soon enough it was evident that they only wanted me for the political influence they thought the Kaspari family would have. And we don't have that much. We can't influence what the assembly says, even if we have ties with many of the members. We of the Kaspari family may be eccentric and the subject of gossip and jokes, but we're not in the business of foul deals and standover tactics." He met Tina's eyes. "That's the only thing I want you to believe about my family. You can ridicule them for their affairs and stupid parties, and some of them heartily deserve it. You can accuse them of being so rich, they don't know what to do with their money. You can accuse them of being out-of-touch. I won't mind. But they are not dishonest and have nothing to do with crime."

A heavy silence followed his words.

Tina let out a deep breath. Why did people have to have such complicated lives? "All right. But that doesn't change the fact that we need supplies and we need to wait in that office. I suggest that we retain our place in the queue. We need to behave like a commercial vessel as much as possible. And that is only until we can figure out what to do next. I'm sure that between all of us we can figure out a way to get our supplies sooner, but to demand them in a room full of people has probably been tried before, and I am not sure I'd like to hear about the result of that."

Finn hung his head. "I'll volunteer to take over from Rex," he said.

"But you were so afraid to go into the station," Tina reminded him.

"Someone has to do it."

"I can do it," Rasa said.

Both Finn and Tina said "No," at the same time.

Rasa snorted, as if she couldn't see their objection. "I used to do this all the time. Most of the ships hire a little boy or girl who does this sort of stuff. Nobody ever gives them any attention."

Tina did remember seeing lots of young people in the queue. "I've seen that other ships do this. We need to look inconspicuous. I've bought some clothes for Rasa, so she can dress herself and we will do her hair and make her look nice like she is proper ship's crew."

Finn had to admit defeat. "Well then, let's all keep our heads down and say nothing, and do nothing unusual, and hope to high heaven that we can get through and that nobody discovers us here."

It left the problem of money. Finn might be from a rich family, but he hadn't given any indication that he could help out in the money department.

Tina asked him about it. "Is there a possibility that you or your family could give me some money to facilitate the process?"

Finn shook his head. "If you pay extra money to have your case given priority, you're effectively paying a bribe, and you raise awareness. It's one thing to come here and play dumb, it's another to go and break all kinds of rules. That's just asking for trouble."

"But they don't need to know the money came from you."

"No, but once you start donating as much money as they usually require, you're sure to come under a lot of scrutiny."

It made a lot of sense, and Tina assumed that he had a lot more experience with things like this than she had at Gandama, where small bribes usually worked. "But what about some help with docking fees and all that? I'll pay it back." After she had deducted his share.

"My father has control over my accounts."

"What? You're an adult."

"It's very common in families like ours. They don't trust the younger generation until they're properly settled, and know they're not going to marry a vindictive partner who is only in it for the money. My father says I already proved that can be an issue. My father thinks I'm a failure, and he doesn't know that I've left the Force."

Ouch.

They still needed money, so Tina spent some time looking around for something she could sell. Goose eggs were the best thing she could come up with, but they weren't very expensive.

She also had her collection of cactuses.

But she very much doubted that people here would care much about them. Even if they were also the result of a rift infection.

CHAPTER TEN

TINA LEFT the ship with Rasa and went through the checkpoint and the crowded hall again to get to the office.

Rex waited patiently, surrounded by pretty much the same people who had been there before. Now that she paid attention, Tina did notice quite a number of scruffy-looking young people in the room.

"Look, I've progressed a whole ten numbers," Rex said.

"And how many numbers are there? Four hundred?"

Rex grinned.

"Rasa is here to take over from you. She says it's common that captains get junior crew or pay kids to wait on their behalf. We agreed that it's best to do as other ships do. Rasa said she's done this before, and that this is what ships do."

"Will you be all right?" Rex said. He looked concerned.

"Don't worry about me, I'm going nowhere."

"I wonder why all this queueing is necessary?" Rex said. "Even in Gandama we can do most of these things online."

"They used to do that in most of the stations, too," Tina said. "Until they found far too much abuse of the system, so they needed to insist that every person actually shows their face in the office to make sure that the ship exists and that all the papers are in order. It's far too easy to falsify electronic records."

"I'm sure there are better solutions."

"Yes, but they're also much more expensive."

"The queues are just a way to get people in here and sell them stuff while they're waiting," Rasa said. "Or take their pictures and scope out who they are. Another reason to hire someone to do it, someone who is unimportant and has no marks against their name."

Tina and Rex left Rasa in the office. They walked back through the main hall where it was just as busy as before, regardless of the time of day.

"This is a bit like Kelso, but bigger and with more problems," Rex said.

"Stations are nasty. They're not friendly for individuals, and it is very easy to disappear. That's why I wanted to come to the largest station, so that we have more chance of staying undetected." She then told Rex all the things Finn had said about his family and about the reward for a cure against the infection."

His eyes widened. "Really? And he says his family isn't in it for the money?"

"When you're as rich as they are, two million credits is probably not enough to pay your monthly grocery bill."

"But I thought you said he didn't like his family and he wasn't working for them any more."

"Liking and not working for are two entirely different things. I don't think he's working for them directly. Apparently his family doesn't know that he's bombed out of the Force. I don't like his keeping secret that there was a reward for the cure and that he was married to the station director, but I think he was embarrassed about it, rather than that he deliberately hid it from us."

"Do you think all of this could have anything to do with that paper you sent away for publication?"

"That's what I've been wondering. I think it's drawn attention to me. To us. I'm sorry."

A group of workers in ship overalls came the other way. It must be the end of a mining shift. Tina and Rex weaved their way between them.

"So what arrangements did you make with your friend?" Tina asked when they got back together.

"He wants to see us now," Rex said.

"Did he tell you where he lives?"

"He said he'd meet us in the hall."

From the first gallery level in the atrium, they looked out over the heads of the people on the ground floor. There were hundreds and hundreds of people here.

"Do you know what he looks like?"

"I don't, but there he is," Rex said.

He was looking at the screen on his arm.

It displayed a red dot over a young man who was weaving through the crowd and coming in their direction.

As Tina and Rex stood watching him, he stopped and looked up. It turned out he was just underneath the balcony.

He was much younger than Tina expected. He was thin and lanky, pale-skinned with elfin-like blond hair.

"How old is this kid?" Tina asked.

"Hey, I'm sixteen. You said I was an adult. He's a year older. You can't call him a kid."

He looked like a kid. He even carried one of those ubiquitous kid-weapons, a catapult, in his pocket. "And he knows how to fix ships?" Tina's hope of getting a cheap fix job evaporated before her eyes.

"He doesn't, although he could probably do a decent job, but it's his dad who does the work."

All right. His dad sounded a bit better.

They took the stairs down, meeting Jens on the ground level. The kid wore baggy, much-used clothes that were at least one size too big for him. All of his clothing was dark, either black or some variation of black. His most notable feature was his startling light-blue eyes.

"Hi," Rex said.

The boy said, "Hi."

And then they stood in a kind of awkward silence.

"You're Jens?" Tina asked.

"I am."

And then there was another awkward silence

These boys never expected to see each other. They certainly hadn't expected to see one another in her presence. Mothers did really spoil a lot of teenage fun, simply by being present.

Jens was taking in Rex and his armour. He smiled. "That's really awesome."

"Thanks," Rex said. "But you have to credit my mother, because she got it for me at Kelso."

The eerie light blue eyes took her in. "That's so awesome. What can you do with it?"

"I'm still discovering."

And that was true. Every day, Rex discovered new things he could do with his harness.

Jens again looked at Tina. "Rex tells me that you have a shop where you sell all this cool security equipment?"

"I do."

That was the first time her shop had been mentioned in this way.

"He tells me that you managed to get a box of Hirsh-94 3D sensors."

"I did, but we sold some of them."

"I can imagine. They're so awesome. You can't imagine what you can do with them."

Tina felt a pang of regret. Life was so simple at Gandama, and when—or if—she ever came back, the shop would no longer be there.

The sensors, though, she hadn't been able to bring herself to leave in dusty Gandama, and they were back at the ship. Minus the two she'd sold.

"We need an inverter fixed," Tina said. "We have a large-systems engineer on board, but no one who's an expert in electronics."

"My dad's amazing. He's the one who does the fixing. Come, I'll take you to him."

They started walking through the corridors. Tina made sure she had her tracker turned on, because she wanted to know where they were.

Rex and Jens had gotten over their awkwardness and were now asking each other about others in their group. At first they spoke in soft voices, and then they laughed and spoke more freely.

Rex asked about all the people Jens had met of their community, and Jens said some of them lived on the station, but he didn't know who they were, and some were friends he saw quite regularly. It depended how much he trusted the people whether he wanted to meet them, because you had to be careful.

Compared to him, Rex had grown up in a very isolated

environment. His contact with his technology groups was the only thing that kept him tied with other young people. Rex possibly trusted too many people.

And she had been trying to limit the amount of time he spent chatting to them. That's what parents did: they drew you away from friends and fun things to make you do dumb tasks like clean up your room, and then they dared accuse you of not being social enough.

Yeah, things you'd never thought you'd say to your kids.

They arrived at a residential area. Sometimes the apartment doors stood open, and sounds of talking, smells of cooking, and music drifted out. Little children ran around playing games in small courtyards.

This was a type of station area that Tina had rarely seen.

Jens turned to one of the doors. He unlocked it by pressing the palm of his hand against the lock—an unusually tight security arrangement that was not evident in any of the units around them.

He opened the door.

Tina half expected to go into a dark apartment with a few blinking lights and electronics spread all over the floor and tables, but the apartment was clean and light-filled.

"Hi Dad, I've brought them," Jens said.

They went into the room. At the dining table sat a man who was almost a copy of his son, except a number of years older. He wore very dark glasses that made it impossible to see his eyes.

"This is my father, Thor."

For a man called Thor Olafsen, this man looked as unlike a Norse god as one could imagine. He was as tall and thin as his son, he looked very frail, and Tina was quite sure that behind his dark glasses his eyes would be clouded with white, most likely through laser damage.

And he fixed equipment?

"Sit down," he said, his voice surprisingly warm.

Tina and Rex sat and the man got up, found his way unerringly across the room, and poured some cups of boiling water. Also without searching he found some tea powder, put the lot onto a tray and brought it to the table.

Maybe he wasn't blind after all.

"My son tells me you want something fixed."

"That's true. We need the main inverter fixed on the ship. We have continuous power problems. I'm not sure what sort of payment you expect in return. Unfortunately, I can't offer a lot of money."

"Hmmm. Thank you for being up-front about that. Money is not terribly useful here. Everyone has buckets of it, but there is not much to buy. Maybe you can offer some useful items, like more interesting food than the station stores give us?"

"We've also come to buy supplies. Ours have run down, because we started our journey with more people than we anticipated. We've only got curry."

He pulled a face and everyone laughed.

Then Tina said, "I may have some things on board the ship to interest you."

"Oh? Do you think this could be interesting?" The latter to his son. He didn't turn his head, which convinced Tina that he was, indeed, almost completely blind.

"I think so," Jens said.

"And it's something that isn't going to get you into trouble with authorities, like that weapon of yours?"

"The catapult?" Jens laughed. "That's only a toy, remember?"

"Right. A toy that can precisely fire magnets attached to a string through a metal barrier so you can pilfer electronic parts from the station stores."

"They wouldn't sell us the connectors."

"Because you're not licensed mechanics. You're boys who can get into a lot of trouble using serious equipment."

"Hmph."

Tina bit her lip. This reminded her so much of the discussions between herself and Rex.

Thor turned back to her. "All right. Let's talk about the money later. My son tells me you've come from Kelso Station."

"We have."

"I've heard they were free until recently."

"Kelso was taken by pirates but has come back to Federacy rule."

"I heard this, too. Are you with pirates, or are you with the Federacy?"

Tina wasn't sure what to say, the way that question was framed. Was she supposed to be with pirates, or was she supposed to hate the pirates?

"We're just commercial traders. I don't really care terribly much about the Federacy or pirates. We just want to complete our job. I'm carrying a passenger to Olympus, but we had some unexpected trouble and needed to stop to have our ship fixed."

He gave a small snort. "If you were a normal business, you would know all the normal procedures for getting your ship fixed on Aurora, and also that it takes a long time."

"I've never been here before," Tina said.

But she also knew that was not a very satisfactory answer.

In fact, he started laughing loudly.

"Do you know that you are terrible liars? Just normal business." He clapped his hand on his knee. "You're about as regular as Fearnley's Comet: comes around every hundred years. Everyone thinks it's something new every visit. Come on then, let me know what needs fixing. Give me some details about the problems you've been having with the ship."

She and Rex explained the problem as much as they were able. He nodded throughout their story.

"That's a known problem with those ships. Take me out there, and I'll be able to fix it. You said you had an engineer? He should have been able to fix this."

"He worked on large ships."

"Hmph. They know everything about nothing. You ask them what they do, and they come up with a fancy name that means they take care of the engine that produces the fart that stops the ship bumping into the docking boom. But only the one on the left-hand of the ship, not the right."

He got up, leaving half of his tea, and started collecting his tools.

He asked his son to get all manner of things, and collected them into a pair of backpacks that looked predesigned for the purpose of carrying their tools. There were a number of hooks on the outside and each held a tool.

Tina looked around the meticulous apartment. Not a thing was out of place. She concluded that his blindness accounted for why everything was so neat.

She sent Finn a small warning message that if he didn't want to be seen by a local, he had better hide in one of the cabins. Was there a chance that Jens had contact with the Partlow family? Who knew?

Tina was happy that at least this part of the mission was going well.

CHAPTER ELEVEN

TINA LED the way back to the ship. She walked at the front while Rex alternated between walking next to her or with his friend Jens who assisted his father by occasionally touching his elbow to warn of obstacles ahead.

It was busy in the passages, with people milling about outside shops and offices, and harassing passersby for money, food or jobs. Jens was busy steering them away from his father and protecting his tool bag, which little urchins insisted they wanted to carry in exchange for money or food.

It only got a little less cramped when they arrived at the big atrium.

"Look, over there," Rex said.

On the other side of the hall, over the heads of a mass of people seated on bags, stood a couple of men. They were tall and broad-shouldered and wore dark jackets made from a thick material and broad belts with loops that held various knives, clubs and other weapons. Real pirate belts.

One of the men displayed a glint of metal in the space between his shoe and trouser leg where he clearly had an artificial leg. Another man had mottled grey skin. He carried two guns and a stunner.

"That's the first pirates I've seen," Rex said.

"Even all the time you've been waiting in the office?" Tina asked.

"Yes. All the people there make a real effort to tell everyone they're not pirates."

"They're trouble. Don't catch their attention," Thor said.

"Those men can see and hear a lot of things that normal people can't," Jens said. "You have to be careful around them."

"You mean they have enhancements?" Tina asked.

"I've never seen any electronic ones," Jens said. "They're just very dangerous people. I had a friend who was walking in a group a couple of rows back from one of these characters, and he said something, and the toad just turns around and whacks him in the face with those dangly bits that hang off his chin. It made a red welt on his forehead. He's still got the mark. It's turned brown now, but it happened a few months back."

"Do they often attack people?" Rex asked.

"Only when you're trying to be smart," Jens said.

"They go for the kids and the other weaker people," Thor said. "They're cowards, sowing fear within the poor classes so they won't start a rebellion or help Federacy troops."

When they came back to the ship, Finn sat at the table.

He got up as soon as they came in and greeted Jens and his father. "I'm David," he said.

He looked sideways at Tina while he said this, warning her he didn't want to be called by his real name.

Tina said, "This is Jens and his dad Thor. He's a mechanic and is willing to have a look to see if he can fix our inverter. Why don't you show him where it is?"

Finn preceded the pair down the narrow ladder into the maintenance shaft that held the electronics.

Tina remained at the top, looking down on the small space, which grew very crowded with three people in it.

"Do you know these ships well?" Finn asked.

"I know all the ships," Thor said. "There is not one I haven't taken apart and put back together." He ran his hands over the control board.

Finn looked up, frowning at Tina. No doubt he was wondering how Thor could do this work while blind.

Tina shrugged. She saw no reason to distrust Thor, but she couldn't explain all that in one look.

Thor opened the electronics panels. He removed two panels and set them on the floor beneath the openings, but kept the third one attached to the wall so that it made a table. As he removed circuit boards from the inside, he placed them on this makeshift table in a neat grid. Each time he used a tool, he put it back in the same position in his belt.

He extracted a device from his bag that tested currents. It came with an earpiece that he clipped on. A tinny computerised voice called out readings as he probed each circuit board and slotted the ones he tested and found in order back into the cabinet.

Eventually, he was left with one panel.

"Just as I thought," he said. "These chips burn out really quickly."

He retrieved his backpack—which he had placed under the makeshift table—and produced a foldable heatproof surface and a battery-operated heat gun. He turned the offending circuit board upside down and, with a few quick moves and a blast of air from the gun, removed the chip.

A clear plastic box from inside his pack contained an

assortment of chips. He ran his fingertips across the top of each package until he found what he needed, unwrapped the replacement chip and slotted it into the board, which he replaced in the cabinet.

"Can you turn off umbilical power?" he asked.

Tina went to the controls and turned off the mains.

The light flickered and then came on again. Great. Tina went back to the top of the ladder.

Finn said, "Well, that obviously worke—"

The light flickered off. Darkness.

Thor's voice came from below her. "Hmm. I may need to take this one in for a closer look. You said you hadn't run the ship for many years?"

"Fifteen."

"Hmm. I'm surprised it works as well as it obviously has to get you here. These old boats are tough."

Tina didn't say anything about nearly missing the jump window.

Rex produced a light from the tip of his metal fingers and shone it down the ladder, but, being blind, Thor had already pulled the board back out.

Tina switched back to umbilical power. The light came back on.

Thor shut all the covers and carefully put the circuit board into his pack, all without once asking for assistance.

"Since I ripped out the power feed because it's on the circuit board, you'll probably have to reload the software. I'm an electrician, not a computer person. You'll have to find someone else to do that."

"It's all right. I can do that myself," Tina said.

"Are you sure?"

"I am an expert in installing and fixing security systems. I reboot electronic systems all the time."

"Hmm, that's interesting."

He asked her about the work and her shop while he packed up his tools and zipped up his backpack, and then produced a tiny battery-operated vacuum cleaner and swept up the little bits of wire casing and bits of metal he'd dropped on the ground.

"I know these little specks of rubbish can create a lot of trouble once you cast off from the station."

Then he was done and came back up the ladder, followed by his son who carried the packs.

"Why don't you make some tea?" Tina said to Rex.

She, Finn and Thor sat down at the table in the main cabin. It was time to talk business. "How much do we owe you?" Tina asked.

"I normally charge two hundred—"

Tina stifled a gasp. "I have things I can trade. Just not a lot of money."

"I'd be happy with a favour."

"It depends on what it is."

"I want you to take my son to a safe place when you leave the station."

"No, Dad, you're coming, too."

"I can't."

"I've told you several times it's not worth it. She's dead."

Thor shook his head. "I won't leave until I know. This place isn't safe for you. I want you to go."

"It's not safe for you either! I want you to come."

A heavy silence hung in the cabin. Jens looked in anguish at his father. His father's expression remained blank.

"The boy's mother left a long time ago," Thor said by way

of explanation. "Leaving me alone to look after him. Alone and blind." He gave a mirthless chuckle. "I found a new friend. A very good lady friend. When the pirates came to the station, she was at work. She works in the hospital." He paused. "A real good lady. She didn't come home that day, or the day after, or the day after that. I asked the hospital but no one was taking my calls. Nobody has seen her since. The hospital is on the other side of the wall, so we can't go there."

"Wall?"

"They closed off parts of the station where no one can go. There are sections of public space, like the farms and the schools, where no one has been for a long time. No one who was in that area has come back or has been heard from since the walls went up."

"How many people are we talking about?"

"This list of people officially missing has eighty thousand names, but it's likely that some got off the station and no one knows where they are, and other names are not on the list but they should be, because entire families have gone missing and there is no one left to report them."

"Does anyone know why that area in the station was closed?"

"No one does. No one can go there."

Tina glanced at Rex. What about that tea?

He went into the hallway, taking Jens with him, to get extra cups from storage. They spoke in low voices.

Thor detailed how he had looked for his lady friend and had then met up with other people who were also missing family members or friends.

At that moment, there was a shout—Jens?

Rex called out, "No, not that door!"

But it was too late.

Two geese ran into the cabin, squawking loudly. Another flew low over their heads, almost hit the table, and landed in a heap on one of the passenger seats. The goose scrambled to its feet and walked away, indignantly waggling its tail.

The other two stood at Finn's feet, eying him up. Finn had pressed himself as far back in his seat as he could. He was this close to jumping up onto the seat, so the geese couldn't reach his trouser legs.

"Who opened that door?" Tina said.

"Jens did by accident. We'll catch them."

Rex managed to catch two geese with great agility. They could bite his hands as much as they wanted, but that didn't affect Rex at all.

The third one, though, remained elusive. Every time Rex came close, it took flight. Tina looked on in despair, and half-ducked when it came over, as the goose was a big bird and didn't have much room to fly. But look at all that fluff coming down in the cabin! They had just spent a long time cleaning all the dust from disuse. They didn't need any more dust.

Rex chased after it. "Stop, stop. Come here, you stupid bird."

"Better not let Rasa hear that," Tina said.

Eventually, the goose settled on top of a support beam that ran through the cabin, in between the outlet of the air vent and the duct that held the electronics. It sat there out of reach, looking down with a beady eye.

"What do we do now?" Rex asked.

"It will come down when it gets hungry," Tina said.

She wasn't so sure of that, because Rasa was the one who knew most about how to handle the geese but she would return later.

A sense of calm returned to the cabin.

Thor chuckled. "I was going to say something, but I completely forgot what we were talking about."

"You were talking about the pirate occupation," Tina said. "How they closed off half the station. Do you know what goes on there?"

His expression went dark. "Officially, we don't. They even fail to acknowledge that the section is closed."

"What's the station director's standpoint on this?" Tina asked. She glanced at Finn. "Surely she knows and she must have some communication with the pirates."

"She's useless. You can lodge a complaint to her, and she says she'll look into your question, but she never does."

"Would she have signed agreements with the occupiers to keep quiet in return for being left alone? Do you think she even knows what goes on in the rest of the station?"

"Of course she does. It's not terribly hard to make a pretty good guess. Show them, son."

Jens pulled out his diagnostics screen, and with a few taps of his fingers, brought a graphic to it which displayed the shape of the station. With another touch on the screen, the station became divided into red and green sections. Tina thought she recognised the entry to the docks at the very edge of the green section.

"All that red area is off-limits?"

"You got it."

"So how does this show what goes on there?"

Thor said, "Humans need heat, right? And humans produce heat. We can measure heat. One of the first things you learn in space rescue and space warfare: if it doesn't produce heat, it's dead and not worth your energy."

Tina nodded. She had heard that crude observation.

"Well, look at this." He flicked his fingers at Jens, who

changed the image. It was now in black-and-while, an infrared image of the station, possibly taken from an off-site satellite. How did he get access to this?

It showed the station as a bunch of grey circles floating in space. Each of the circles was marked with lighter mottling.

"I can't see the difference between the two sections anymore," Tina said. She could still see the docking structures, because some of the ships produced bright spots of extreme heat, especially the larger ones.

"That's just the point. There is no difference in the occupation level. We know how crowded we are in here, so they have to keep an equal density of people in the restricted section, which means they've had to bring in extra people."

"What with? I only saw a couple of small pirate ships in the docks. Nowhere near the capacity to move a serious number of people."

"Large ships come every now and then. Like the massive troop carriers."

She asked, "Not like the SS *Stavanger*?"

"Exactly like that."

"Do people see those ships arrive?" Tina found it hard to believe.

"They usually close the docks when those ships are here. But I know about troop carriers. I can hear when they come to the station by the way the floor vibrates when a really big ship attaches."

"They close the docks? Does that mean no one can leave or arrive?"

"Yeah, but if you're afraid of getting stuck, they usually clear out everyone they can get rid of beforehand. A lot of the people who are waiting at the port authority or supply office suddenly get permission to leave and get supplies."

Yes, people in the Ship Supply office had also been talking about this.

"So is that when they're bringing in extra people?"

"Yeah. More likely they're transporting prisoners. That's the only way the population of the station would increase that much. That, and the ones who go missing."

"Wait, people still go missing?"

"All the time. Not as many as before. Most of them are young kids, often when they're seventeen, eighteen. That's why I want you to take Jens. He's getting to that age. I don't know when we'll next have the chance."

"But you're coming, too, Dad."

"I'm not going to have this discussion again. You're leaving with these people when they have permits and supplies to travel. I'll join you later."

A few moments of tense silence followed, in which Jens glared at his father, but one of the advantages of being blind was that Thor couldn't see this, so he just cradled his cup in his hands, his face relaxed, oblivious to his son's angry stare.

Tina asked, "Do you know much about the pirates? Do they have a leader? Where did they come from?"

"We don't see much of them. They're not that interested in the people they don't want to use. We see them occasionally, but everything I know is from things I've heard. They don't mingle with us. They don't talk to us. Their leader is a man call Artan, who, according to some records, used to have a relationship with the Federacy."

"Have you seen him?"

"No, but all kinds of stories go around about him, including that he looks like a walking toad. I don't know what to believe. Artan is a man who used to be called Jackson Hirsh. He used to be the Federacy Assembly representative for one of the settled worlds. He was always very outspoken and had a lot of ideas, but most of the representatives weren't too keen on him. They found him too radical. He wanted to put the bases and worlds under civilian control and wanted to install assemblies for each of them. He had lots of big ideas, but was always stifled by the Assembly. He got frustrated."

"Why did he go to the pirates then?" Tina asked. "Has he always been a leader? I thought pirates didn't have leaders."

"Many still don't. Many still live in their shipworld communities."

"That's actually still a thing?" Rex asked. "Not just something from the stories?"

"Yeah, it's a real thing. They have a medium-sized ship, which houses thirty to fifty crew, and travel wherever they like and harvest, collect or steal whatever they can find."

"And do they actually hijack other ships in mid-space?" Rex's eyes were wide.

"Not as often as they used to. It's risky business and there are much easier ways of stealing money, but it still happens."

"Whoa."

"I heard rumours about how the pirate communities changed a number of years ago," Tina said. "Do you know anything about that?"

"Yeah. It must have been about ten years ago when the delegate Jackson Hirsch just disappeared from Olympus. No one knew where he had gone at the time. It was a big scandal. Don't you remember it?"

"No. I've been out of touch for a long time."

"It was a big thing. He disappeared and, after a while, they stopped looking for him. Later these pirate armies started to appear, where two or more shipworlds had come together and formed a larger group. They never used to work together and now they did. And doing so gave them better and longer-lasting victories. The pirates wanted worlds and stations to live on, for their families, because living in small ships was not very good for the health of their population. There were children born in those craft. Many of the ships are so old they don't even have rotating habitats. Artificial gravity is only derived from constant acceleration or deceleration. Those conditions are terrible for adults, let alone growing children and developing babies. The Federacy wouldn't let the Freerangers set up bases on worlds or stations, so they banded together and took them by force. But I thought all of it was quite well-known."

"I only heard this recently." Tina grew quite annoyed with herself. She had let herself drop out of connection with everyone, and in running her shop at Gandama, she had not kept up with the news from anywhere within the Federacy. If only she had done that, she might have realised that trouble was brewing long before now. Then again, what could she have done about it? She tried, and Dexter still sold material to the pirates.

Thor announced it was time for them to go home. Jens wanted to stay, but his father said that it was best not to draw attention to themselves until they brought back the inverter.

They went to the door to the access tube, but before they left the cabin, Finn asked Thor, "Did you ever serve in the Force?"

Thor laughed. "Did I serve? I was their star missile technician."

A silence passed in which someone should have asked "But what happened?" but didn't. Yet everyone looked at his dark glasses, which, in turn, he couldn't see.

He continued, "That was until some dickhead switched on

the high-intensity laser while I was working on it. Burned my eyes. I was thirty three. They retired me after that, but I didn't want their pity, so I struck out on my own. Learned to do the work without my eyes."

He was a brave fellow. Tina liked him.

When Thor and Jens had gone, Tina did some research on Jackson Hirsh. Pictures from his time in the Federacy Assembly showed him as a friendly-faced man with a thoughtful expression. He was supposed to look like a toad now?

His employment record showed that he'd been a public servant for his entire career. He'd never been in the Force, never been to Project Charon or even Pandana. He wasn't listed in any need-to-know lists for Federacy Force research, or indeed any kind of advice or emergency council.

But her very last check delivered a surprise: he'd been at the meeting where Dexter had passed his materials to the pirates.

Well, that was interesting, although he looked to have been there as admin staff, and there was no record of meetings that involved him, and indeed his name was never mentioned in any of the meeting's reports.

Very interesting.

Tina got up to make some tea.

The one stray goose was waddling down the hallway, looking for a way back into the cabin where it could hear its companions. Tina went to open the door. It waddled through and flew on top of the cage.

Tina shook some grain into the bird feeder and opened the door when the four geese in the cage were crowding around the tray. The fifth goose joined them.

She noticed some spots on its back.

Strange. Tina was sure all geese were completely white. It must have brushed against something dark, because there were some golden spots on its back. Now she was worried because it looked like oil, and she hoped to hell nothing up there in the sloping roof cavity of the cabin was leaking, because a lot of the vital driving and stabilising mechanism of the habitat's rotation system went through there.

"Have you noticed any drops of oil on the floor in the last few days?" she asked Finn when she came back into the cabin.

"No, why?" Finn asked.

"Just keep a lookout for any." Damn, she hoped that mechanism wasn't going to blow up, too. That would make their trip to wherever extremely unpleasant.

Rex had ensconced himself inside the navigation cubicle with the computers.

"I'm going to make some tea," she announced.

He nodded, not looking up from the screen.

"What are you doing?" Tina asked him.

"Checking out some of the stuff Jens showed us."

"Getting into satellite recordings?"

"I don't know. I'll see what I can find."

Tina went to the kitchen at the back of the cabin.

"Security is pretty lax," he commented a bit later. "It's easy to get into a lot of stuff."

"Don't get us into any more trouble than we already are," Tina warned.

"They don't even use double-checking protocols."

"I find that hard to believe." That was pretty standard for security procedures even on the backward world of Gandama.

"I'm not kidding. Come and have a look at this," he said.

She went into the cubicle, where he had flipped out the table so that he could use it as a stand for his projector.

It displayed a long list of what looked like a supply order. Tina was familiar with those, because you needed to fill those out if you wanted to buy something in the Force. That sort of information was not normally open to the public.

This one contained all manner of chemical components.

"What is this?" she asked.

"I don't know, but it says 'confidential' at the top."

It did, too. Tina wondered why a supply order for chemicals was confidential. They were pretty standard lab supplies. "What would they do with this?"

But no one could answer that question.

CHAPTER TWELVE

BEFORE HAVING A VERY LATE DINNER, Tina went to the Ship Supply office to check with Rasa. The floor of the room had been turned into a camp, with sleeping mats and even blow-up mattresses spread over the floor. They were all placed in neat rows with room to walk in between. The people's bags sat on the seats where people waited during the day. People sat or lay on their makeshift beds. Two children in pyjamas made their way out of the room carrying a small bag with what Tina assumed to be toiletries.

Tina found Rasa close to the side of the room, sitting on a mat, talking to a middle-aged woman and a man Tina assumed to be the woman's husband.

The couple both looked up when Tina approached, and Rasa, with her back to the door, turned around.

"It's my turn," Tina said. "Go back to the ship to get some dinner."

"I've already eaten. The people here are really nice. They're all from the ships and they all know each other and help each other—Hanna, this is my captain, Tina."

"Hi." The woman smiled at Tina, a bit awkward.

Rasa got to her feet. "You don't need to take my spot. This is what the junior crew does. These people are all junior crew or passengers who have agreed to sit here in return for a cheap fare. Captains don't wait here."

"You're sure?"

"Yes, sure. You see those men over there?"

Rasa glanced over her shoulder at the men who stood on either side of the door, as if they were waiting. They were big burly types and, although not in uniform, looked and acted like guards.

"They're keeping an eye on everyone in here. I've already seen how they stopped some older boys harassing a younger one. They don't want trouble. They don't want fights to break out here. It's safe. I haven't seen any pirates. No one has talked any of that kind of stuff to me. No one unfriendly leastways."

So Tina returned to the ship, where she found Rex and Finn together in front of the computer.

"I told you she wouldn't want to come," Finn said without looking up from the screen.

"At least she can't accuse me of not offering."

"Those offices are the safest places to be in the stations," Finn said. "If she has to be somewhere in the station, that's the best place."

Tina didn't agree but there was no point in arguing. She made some tea and watched Finn and Rex from the bench in the cabin. Whatever they had found sounded interesting, though, so she looked over their shoulders.

Rex had broken into another database, and had pulled up maps of the vast station, with areas where the public was allowed to go and areas where they weren't. This was not a heat scan, but a highly detailed map of the sections of the station and all its rooms, labelled with their functions. She spotted the hospital that Thor had spoken of, and the school.

Rex and Finn had also discovered an area that might function as the pirate control centre on the third level of the school, which contained a staff meeting room. It was well within the closed section of the station. They had managed to intercept a number of messages that originated from this area—a room on the upper floor—which appeared to be instructions about operations of the station and the delivery of goods. Exactly what was being delivered wasn't clear—Finn suggested chemical supplies necessary for operation of the air scrubbing plant. It seemed at least someone had an interest in keeping the station operational.

Which, in a station this size, was not a small undertaking and required a certain level of organisation to achieve.

It was a good sign, right?

"Do you see anything that supports the theory that they've turned the other half of the station into a prison or holding pen?" she asked Rex.

He shook his head. "We don't have that type of heat scanner."

"Where did Jens' data come from?"

"He said a hacked satellite. I don't know where to find that data."

But they intercepted a news channel. Apparently, the pirate leader called Artan used Aurora as a base.

There was also quite a lot of discussion of disagreements between factions, "shipworlds" as Thor called them, although the term seemed to belong to the romantic world that her parents had grown up in as settlers on Tirkala. Whatever they were called, the pirates held autonomy of these small units in very high regard.

Artan's actions were breaking down this autonomy. Many of the older pirate groups were not happy.

The entry page of the news service had what looked like a permanent feature on the pirate leader Artan. His pirate-sanctioned biography listed information from his time at the Assembly. A petition for autonomy of Palinda, a world where a lot of technology was developed. A proposal for redefinition of the scientific good. She could see what Finn meant about his ideas being too radical for the stodgy Federacy Assembly.

He'd been a product of the restrictions of the political bureaucracy, not that this justified violent action against the Federacy. Not at all.

And the devotion of his fans within the pirate world bordered on religious. The news bulletins even contained children's poems written for him. They were about freedom. What was this lack of freedom they were supposed to have had under Federacy rule? Was it worse than having many people go missing, lacking supplies or being unable to leave the station?

With the promise of new ship supplies some time in the future—whenever Rasa got to the front of the queue—they needed to finish up the old ones, and dinner consisted of an odd combination of prepacked meals, because it would be a waste to let it go off or discard the packages. Also because Tina didn't feel like going out again and buying food.

Then she spent a restless night thinking about Rasa and her easy-going personality that made her friends with everyone. She worried about Rex and what sort of world he was going to grow up in if pirates with few morals were going to play a major role in it.

The ship was very quiet when the engines were off, and she was left listening to the creaks and clicks of the station and the movement of ships docking and undocking. Thor had said that he could hear it when a large ship docked. She could believe it.

The geese chattered in the cabin across the hallway. It was surprising how much she noticed the absence of Rasa, who had shared the cabin with her for the past few days since they stowed the habitat.

Somehow, she had a feeling that someone was watching them and laughing at their terrible efforts to hide themselves.

She got up early in the morning, sick of tossing and turning, and found Rex already in the kitchen. He had extended his harness even further, and now he was much taller than her, a truly impressive sight of gleaming metal machinery. If anything good had come out of this hare-brained trip, Rex's newfound confidence—the fact that he was now independent and no longer needed to rely on her—was the best. He'd found inner peace and lost his angry reaction to everything.

When Tina commented on the tallness of the harness, he said that he wanted to get some weapons extensions, so that he could make use of its full capabilities. He was still learning new features.

Tina felt cold at the idea that her son was turning into a fighting machine. He was too young to face violence.

They left the ship to see how Rasa was doing and whether she needed anything. The crowd still stood at the gate into the docks, hurling questions at Tina when they passed.

"I wonder if these people ever get what they want?" Rex asked after they had cleared the checkpoint.

"They're probably so hopeless that waiting here is all they can do."

It was a world that was strange to her. She knew these things happened, because she had travelled to stations where she had seen these people return day in day out to the same area, hoping that someone would give them a job, a lift off the place or scraps of food.

It had never been clear to her what stations usually did with these people. She wouldn't be surprised if they were being shipped off to a planet as soon as the opportunity arose. But there was no nearby world to Aurora.

Once in the Ship Supply office, they saw that the makeshift beds had all been cleared and the waiting had resumed.

Except they couldn't find Rasa in the queue. Rex looked around over the heads of the many people.

"Can you see her?" Tina's heart was thudding. Something happened to Rasa. They shouldn't have left her overnight.

But then Rex said. "There she is, over there, in that room."

To the side of the main waiting area was another room behind a wall of glass. Inside the room stood easy chairs and screens to watch the news. People sat talking to each other in a relaxed fashion, while someone in a station authority uniform circulated around with a computer.

"It's some kind of VIP area," Rex said.

"How did she end up there?"

Rasa spotted them, got up from her seat and came to the door. "Come in."

The room felt fresher and smelled nicer than the large waiting area. Food sat on the table, and the smell of coffee hung in the air. Real coffee. Not that fake stuff.

"You want some?" Rasa said.

Before Tina could reply, Rasa went to a little bar in the corner, where she helped herself to three cups of coffee, some biscuits and pieces of toast.

"How did you end up here?" Tina asked.

"Contacts," Rasa said.

"How do you get contacts when you live in the docks at Kelso Station?"

"Are you kidding? That's the place you get contacts. The docks. Everybody who travels through comes through the docks. People who travel have money. If you help them, they're happy to help you out. They have these wonderful rooms, but what's the point of it if they can't share and they can't boast about their existence."

"So what? You helped someone? What with?"

Rasa held up another device. "I'm in the line for two ships now. Yes, I'm being paid for it. You said we needed money. People who want to leave stations and are frustrated have money. All you need to do is smile at people and win their trust."

Tina was beginning to feel distinctly duped. Everyone on this trip was smarter than she was. And Rasa was really good at this stuff.

"Anyway, I won't need to stay here very long, because it will be our turn soon. They gave me a list of all the papers they said we needed to sign and told me how much it costs to supply the ship.

"And how much is that?" Deep dread settled in Tina's stomach, because the subject of money was one they hadn't covered up to now.

Rasa said, cheerfully, "Five thousand credits."

"You have got to be kidding."

"No, that's what he said."

"I don't have that much money. I don't have near that much money. At Kelso this costs less than half that amount. That is just a rip-off. And clearly just because you are in this area, and sitting here like a rich person, so they think we have lots of money. I am not paying five thousand credits because I don't have five thousand credits."

As she spoke Tina lowered her voice more and more but other people were listening. Eventually one of the men said, jerking his head at the crowded room on the other side of the glass wall, "That's what they pay out there, too. It's the going rate for this place."

Tina stared at him. "You're kidding, right?"

"No. I wish I was, but I'm not."

Right.

Finn was going to have to pay if he wanted to get out of here. Which, clearly, he did.

She said to Rasa, "I'm going to talk to Finn. Stay here."

"I'm not going anywhere." Rasa put a biscuit in her mouth.

"Come on, Rex."

But Rex wasn't listening at all. He stared at the wall screen. He said in low voice, "Mum."

Tina turned to the wall screen and saw her own face from an ugly, poorly exposed photo taken many years ago when she still worked for Project Charon.

The announcer said, "The situation at Kelso Station has worsened, with the Federacy now taking control of the station again. They have captured our freedom fighters, and have executed a number of our brave soldiers. We are aware that the traitor we came to capture has escaped the station, unfortunately. If you have seen this woman, please do not talk to her or engage her, because she is considered dangerous. She is in possession of important information that may determine our survival. Contact the authorities straight away. If you are watching this, hand yourself over to authorities in orderly fashion. You will not be able to leave this station alive otherwise."

Tina turned away from the screen. People were still watching the announcement, and she didn't think any of them had recognised her. Yet.

"We've gotta get out of here," she said to Rex.

CHAPTER THIRTEEN

"MUM, that was you on the screen," Rex said, while he and Tina walked down the stairs from the Ship Supply Office to the entrance to the docks.

"So I noticed."

"They said you were dangerous."

"All these people here had better get out of our way, then."

"Haha. This is nothing to joke about."

"I'm not joking. You're lucky they didn't show your face as well or say anything about my highly recognisable companion. Keep your head down and don't look so tall and impressive."

"Are you jealous now?"

"I don't want us to be singled out." Because the danger was not in people recognising them but in security cameras recognising her facial profile. Their system security might not be the most modern, but surely the station would have that basic security feature?

But as soon as she and Rex came to the ground floor of the atrium, a lot of cheering went up from near the lifts. A group of people was congregated around a screen.

"What's that about?" Rex asked.

"No idea. I hope something unrelated to us."

They crossed the hall, but even while they passed the checkpoint into the docks and walked the corridors, they noticed a lot of people talking excitedly to each other. People were coming out of doors and getting together in groups. Voices were raised and there was lots of clapping on shoulders. It was disturbing that some of these people looked like pirates.

What was the news? That Kelso Station had been destroyed? That the pirates had invaded the Federacy Assembly?

The upside of the mysterious good news was that nobody paid attention to Tina and Rex as they passed through the corridor.

She turned away from any place she thought a camera might be hiding.

There were so many pirates around all of a sudden. She had never seen that many in this station before. Had they come out of the closed half of the station?

The pirates and associates talked excitedly in groups and many went in the same direction as Tina and Rex: in the direction of where the ships were moored.

Tina waited for a moment to let a big noisy group of them go past, but they just kept coming, and they didn't look at her and Rex at all.

"Something has definitely happened," she said.

"You don't say."

"I wonder what it is."

"It looks like something is going on in this station, and everyone is rushing to have a look."

It was a distraction, and distractions were useful for trying to get away. But it came at the wrong time. Rasa was still in the office, and Tina couldn't see—without knowing what was happening—how they would be able to use the distraction.

She increasingly felt that Finn had been right about the danger of coming here. Aurora was a very high-profile location on the pirates' map. But if she admitted she'd been wrong, Finn would probably gloat over it all the way to Olympus. And that was an awfully long time to listen to his gloating.

Still, more and more people came out of doors and passages and went in the same direction.

The route to the ship went through several lift foyers that gave access to different sections of the docking structures, some for small ships, some for residents of the station, some for large ships. In the largest of these halls, many people crowded around a lift door, watching a screen that hung above the exit.

Many of them were pirates making no secret of what they were, in full outfit. Some wore badges on their jackets, presumably showing to which shipworld they belonged.

A number of them also were people with warty skin. Tina did notice that the interaction between the shipworld pirates and the warty pirates was sparse. They didn't often stand together. They didn't talk to each other.

"It seems it's mainly pirates," Rex said. He could see over the heads of the crowd. "It looks like they're celebrating something."

The giant screen on the wall was now showing a live projection of a ship being docked at the station. This was definitely Aurora Station. The umbilicals were in place, and station staff were opening the access tube doors.

"That looks like a Federacy ship," Rex said in a low voice.

It did, too. Not just that. It *was* a Federacy Force warship. She wasn't sure of the type, because a portion of the ship was obstructed by the station structure, but the top half of the Federacy's crest with the Great Deer constellation was visible on the side.

Tina and Rex got stuck in the crowd, because it was so busy it was impossible to get through. The people around them talked excitedly. From the conversations, it was clear that most were sympathetic to the pirates. The rumour went that the pirate fleet had captured a Federacy Star Fighter. It was the first time it happened, and such a prize it was, too.

"I hope they will let us see inside," one of the people around them said.

"How many crew are in the ship?" someone else asked.

"Yes, how are they going to deal with those people?"

Someone else said, "They'll probably have a public punishment."

"No, they'll give the crew to the farm."

Farm? What farm?

The press of bodies around them grew more intense as people continued to come into the hall.

Several of the warty people took up position behind them.

"Don't look behind you," she told Rex in a low voice. "They might recognise us."

She still felt the prick of their gazes in her neck.

The lift door opened, and people started cheering. A single man came out, raising his hands, balled into fists, above his head. He wore a metal-studded jacket of dark leather, a broad pirate belt with fearsome trophies like an axe and a knife with a huge blade, and knee-high boots. His face was unrecognisable as human, his skin dark red and warty. Long tentacles dangled from the line of his jaw.

He gave a loud cry.

People in the hall cheered.

"What's he saying?" Rex asked. He held up the display on his arm with a translation function enabled, but the shouts and cheers from the crowd yielded nothing except a squiggly line across the display.

A small icon popped up in the corner. "It says it has a positive identification."

"Huh, so it does. You're getting the hang of this, Mum."

Rex touched the corner of the screen. It brought up the picture and information she had already seen: the pirate-sanctioned biography of Jackson Hirsch, or Artan.

People started to push to the sides. The red-skinned pirate was followed by other pirates with grey skin, who set up two lines on either side of a path that formed through the crowd. Tina could see this because Rex flipped out a little step from the side of his leg, and pulled her up so that he could support her while she stood on it.

"Pretty handy," she said.

"Yes, I discovered this the other day when I was helping Finn."

The pirates were followed by a bunch of bedraggled people who were marched into the hall. Their hands were tied behind their backs, their faces were dirty, their uniforms ripped.

Federacy uniforms.

The pirates pushed and kicked these people, some of whom were doing their best just to stay on their feet. They were injured.

The group was paraded through the crowd to much whistling and jeering. They were coming in the direction where Tina and Rex stood, and the pirates at the front of the column motioned the crowd of onlookers aside. Tina and Rex ended up only a couple of rows back from the thoroughfare.

The line started with the formidable figure of the pirate leader. Apart from his dark red skin, he also displayed a veritable garden of growths on his skin, hanging from his jawbone, his ears and neck. His nose had regressed into his face until only two holes remained. His mouth was small and surrounded by dark lips.

Tina made sure that she was not in direct view of him, because she felt that those beady eyes could see everything.

He was followed by a number of his soldiers, each of them pushing a couple of Federacy soldiers in front of them. They were close enough that she could see the emblem on their chests. They were from the Star Fighter *Manila*.

Tina felt cold. That was the ship where her daughter Evelle served.

"Come on, we can get through now," Rex said. He let go of Tina's arm, so that she could descend from her perch to the ground.

But Tina wasn't moving. She hung unto Rex's metallic shoulder and studied the faces of all the captured soldiers who filed past, some injured, most of them looking tired, weary and dirty.

Rex shook his arm. "Come on, Mum."

But Tina still wasn't moving.

Standing out amongst the prisoners was a young woman with spiked up blond hair.

Even though Tina hadn't seen her for almost twenty years, she recognised her face, because a mother never forgets the faces of her children.

It was Evelle.

CHAPTER FOURTEEN

TINA SAW her daughter only briefly.

Her face was pale, with dark smudges and a bruise on her cheek. Her uniform was ripped at the shoulder, showing a red graze on her pale skin, and her hands were tied behind her back. Her weapons had been removed from her belt, but she held her chin high. She looked straight ahead, ignoring all the people who stood on the side, and who either cheered or jeered at the prisoners. She marched past with the column, disappearing into the passage on the other side of the hall.

"Mum, what's going on?" Rex said. "Who are these people? Why is everyone cheering so much?"

Tina said in a low voice, "The pirates have captured one of the Federacy's major warships. Those prisoners are Federacy troops."

The entire group had passed, and everyone had started walking again, even if only slowly.

There were far too many people here and they were far too close for Tina to tell Rex what was going on. She couldn't risk anyone overhearing, at least not any of the many people around here who were sympathetic to the pirates.

Everyone in this crowded hall and crowded passages had become an enemy.

Of course they were that already, but she had always assumed these people to be station citizens, caught between two warring parties and not caring much about either side.

Tina led the way through the passages. The crowds thinned out, so it became easier to move. She set a good pace, and Rex followed her, with his powerful footsteps that went zoom-zoom-zoom each time the harness engaged.

They arrived at the ship, where Finn was down in the engine maintenance compartment. When Tina and Rex entered the main cabin, he came up the steps, wiping his hands on his trousers.

"Shut the door, I have something important to tell you," Tina said to Rex.

She went over to the controls and made sure that none of the recording devices were on.

"Good, now I finally get to know what you're so grumpy about," Rex said.

"Tea?" Finn asked in a mock-cheerful tone. He was in the kitchen at the hot water dispenser.

No one responded.

"Fine. I'm making some anyway." He pulled out some cups, the jar of powdered tea, and proceeded to pour hot water into the cups which he then carried over to the table. Steam rose from the surface.

"Two things have happened." Tina said when they were all seated around the table.

"First of all, for your benefit, Finn, when we came to the Ship Supply office, Rasa was in a different room. She managed to get into the priority queue, and she said she should be able to get a permit to leave the station today."

"She is good, isn't she?" Finn grinned.

"You didn't wait until I got to the part where she said it would cost five thousand credits."

"What?" Finn said.

"I don't have five thousand credits," Tina said. "I spent all my money on trying to do not too badly to the businesses at Kelso Station. My accounts are empty. My credit is maxed out. It looks like we're stuck here unless someone else comes up with some funds."

She looked pointedly at Finn.

"Is Rasa still in the queue?" Finn said, as usual, deflecting the question.

"I left her there, but I'm thinking we may need to retrieve her. When she gets to the end and it turns out that we can't pay, there isn't going to be any point in her staying where she is. I intended to come back to talk to you about that, just in case you might have some money. But on the way back something else happened that, frankly, has thrown doubt over us leaving at all. It seems that the pirates have captured one of the Federacy's Star Fighters. There was a great cheer about it, and when we came to the docks, we saw the crew being led away as prisoners."

Finn's face turned hard. "The poor guys. That's worse than being shot to pieces." His expression was dark.

"Yes. But there is an added complication. One of those crew members happens to be my daughter."

Now Rex whirled to Tina. "What? Evelle? Was she on that ship?"

"She was. When we were at Kelso, I had heard that she

serves on the *Manila*, and I saw her with those prisoners. She looked a bit beaten up, but otherwise proud."

"Did she see you?"

"I don't think so, at least she didn't make eye contact. I wonder whether she would recognise me even if she had seen me."

"You recognised her."

Yes. Evelle would probably recognise her.

"Obviously, it complicates things," Tina said.

Finn met Tina's eyes. "Don't try to be a hero. I don't think there is anything we can do for them. There are far more than one million people on this station, and if most of them are aligned with the pirates, then everyone on this station is going to be our enemy."

"Yes, and they're already looking for us," Rex said helpfully. "Mum's face was in a general broadcast warning."

Tina put her hands flat on the table. "I'm not leaving the station without making sure that my daughter is safe."

"You haven't seen Evelle for sixteen years," Rex said. "You've told me many times that she left, she yelled at you, and she never answered any of your messages."

"She might have been a spoiled brat when she left, but she's still my daughter. I will save her, even if she's a hard-faced bitch without a shred of gratitude. Because I can't expect that piece of shit Dexter to look after her safety. He's not here anyway. I know where she is. I know she is in danger. I will try my best to get her out of that situation."

There was a moment of tense silence, in which both Rex and Finn were wise enough to keep their mouths shut.

After a while, Finn said, "Well, that certainly puts a different perspective on the question of whether we should or should not leave Rasa in the Ship Supply office."

"Exactly. When she gets that permit, we have to act. We have to pay, and we have to leave. Apart from the fact that I have no money to pay, we don't want to leave anymore."

Finn nodded, although his expression was dark. "Are you sure you really want to take on a pirate stronghold?"

"There is no 'want.' I have to do this."

Rex nodded. "You better not interfere with Mum when she gets like this."

Finn didn't, although he heaved a sigh.

Even through all of this, Tina wasn't sure what he had wanted. Get away from his ex, obviously, but what was his relationship to this reward for information leading to the defeat of the rift infection? Was he involved with it? Did he want to use the money to set up independently? If so, was it a good thing for her to be involved in?

But her first concern should be doing what she could for Evelle. She cared much less about going to Olympus anymore. It sounded like too political a place for her liking anyway, and she doubted the stuff that had sat in a document box at Kelso Station for fifteen years was going to make any difference to the Federacy's response to the pirates.

"I want to free Evelle. We need to do something radical," she said.

"You said it," Finn said.

"But what?"

Someone knocked on the inner airlock door.

A male voice said, "Coming to return your inverter panel."

CHAPTER FIFTEEN

TINA WENT to open the door. Jens came in first, looking around anxiously. "No geese today?"

"They're safely tucked away," Rex said, although said geese were making a racket in their cabin.

Thor followed Jens, carrying his bag, which he set on the table and proceeded to take the inverter panel out. "Let's install this baby and see if it works."

Finn went with them into the maintenance access cubicle and clambered down the ladder.

Once he had oriented himself, Thor again needed no help to locate the correct panel cover, and the panel next to it that folded out like a table so he could put his tools there. It was a marvel to behold. He had to know these ships like the back of his hand. He would be such a valuable person to have on board.

When he was done, he asked Tina to turn off the umbilical power.

She did. The light flickered, came back on, and stayed on.

"All done!" Thor called from downstairs.

He replaced the panels, packed his gear and came back upstairs with Finn. Tina invited them to stay for some tea.

"How are you doing for a permit to leave?" Thor asked.

"We're still waiting," Tina said. "Rasa managed to get into a high priority area and should be done today. But the problem is going to be paying for it."

"I wouldn't worry too much about that. It will probably start moving quickly very soon."

"What do you mean? Apparently a ship supply package is five thousand credits."

"Don't worry about it."

"I do worry about it. I don't have anywhere near that kind of money."

"They'll be getting rid of everyone in that room soon, payment or no payment."

Tina remembered what he had said during their previous meeting about closing the docks and secret shipments coming in. "Is there a pirate ship coming in with more prisoners?"

"There is something in the air," Thor said. "I know you don't notice it but when you live here, it's clear when something is about to happen. A new ship arrived. There is excitement in the air. There are many strange people hanging around."

She wondered how he could see this while he was blind. "What sort of people? How do you know?"

"I may not see much, but I got eyes everywhere. People tell me things. Like when groups of men start hanging around the docks. They're pirates, waiting for something to happen, and usually that is the closing of the docks. When that happens, they usually let all the waiting ships leave as quickly as possible, payment or no."

Tina found it hard to believe that they would charge

people five thousand credits and would let others leave without payment, but then again, she had heard about this. Fancy that it might happen to them when they didn't actually want to leave.

"But some ships get to stay?" She had also heard about that.

"No one gets to stay. When they clear out the docks, they literally clear out everyone. Arrivals get told to wait as well."

"But I heard some people say that they waited around."

"Only if the ship really can't be moved. And then they don't allow the crew access to the ships."

Well, crap. She saw herself trying to march five geese into crowded accommodation.

So this left her with little choice. Finn would have to take the ship, hang around the station until the docks opened again and he could come back. Meanwhile she could try to find out where Evelle was... but then she'd have no quick transport off the station if that proved necessary.

"How long does this closure last?"

"A few days usually."

"What happens in the docks when they close?" Something that Rex could break into?

Thor grinned. "Officially, we don't know."

"Officially?"

He waggled his white eyebrows. "We wouldn't go breaking the rules."

"Of course not."

"But if we did, we might have seen people being taken into the agricultural part of the station."

"Which is also off-limits to the general public," Tina guessed. Because those areas usually were closed for fear of contamination.

"That's right. We can only get into the agricultural areas when we have a reason to be there." Again with a waggle of the eyebrows. "Otherwise we might see that they're usually taken through a door at the end that leads past the recycling, where we'd also have no reason to visit."

"Except when it's not working properly and one might be asked to fix something? I've noticed that the air is very stuffy."

"There are never enough people who know the details of how to keep such an intricate recycling plant running properly. The pirates probably don't care about it much, unless it becomes hard to do essential things, like breathe."

"Nor do they have much knowledge about security."

"Nope."

Jens looked from his father to Tina. "What are you two talking about?"

"I think your friend's mother and I understand each other very well. We were both in the Force and we know how to talk about things without actually talking about them."

Jens snorted and glanced at Rex. "Does she do this to you?"

"All the time," Rex said, rolling his eyes.

Now both of them looked from Tina to Thor and back.

Tina said, "But without kidding, do you have anything like the backup for what you're insinuating?" If one could put together a crew to do "maintenance" on the agricultural plant, that was a way to get into the restricted part of the station, because pirate security wasn't terribly good.

"I have, but many people lack the guts and will. They're too afraid they'll go missing as well. They have families to look after. They're cautious."

"Your partner was taken."

He nodded. "I have little left to lose, but I'm just a blind loner. I have friends, but we lack numbers."

"My daughter is crew of the SF *Manila* that was just brought in. I saw her being marched away. She's probably in that restricted area."

Thor sucked in a breath. "I heard about that ship. That's a goldmine of Federacy tech and data right there. I think Artan will be very careful that he doesn't waste the crew's knowledge."

"What do you think he's going to do with them?"

"It's hard to say. We all know something illicit is going on in the other half of the station and that a lot of people live there, but we never see any of them being brought in or taken out and we can only make guesses at what they're doing."

"Which is?"

But a sound at the entrance to the access tube interrupted the discussion. Tina got up to check, finding Rasa in the tube, her face bright.

"I got it."

"What do you mean?"

"We got permission to leave. Stuff will be delivered later."

"But no one has paid anything yet."

"I know. But a man came in and just gave everyone a permit to leave and restock. No one paid anything. They said we would have to carry the supplies ourselves, though. There is some sort of warehouse where we're supposed to pick them up."

"What about fuel?"

"That's getting done right now."

"Without me signing for it and paying?"

"Yup. They seemed in a hurry. They want everyone out."

"See? I told you," Thor said.

Tina met Finn's eyes. He didn't seem to like it much more than she did.

He said to Rasa, "Did you get confirmation that we're allowed to leave?"

"Don't you believe me?"

"I do, but it could be that someone is trying to play a trick on us."

Rasa took the reader that contained the station's ship details, and flicked through a couple of menus. "Here it is." She handed the reader to Finn.

He gave it a look, his face blank. Tina knew that blank look, though. It meant something bothered him. She held out her hand and he passed the reader to her.

Tina read through what appeared to be a pretty normal departure permission note. But she tapped the name at the bottom: Zia Partlow.

"That is the problem," he said.

"She's the station director," Rasa said. She didn't know about Finn's prior relationship with her.

"I know," Finn said, his voice dark. "I'd hoped to never see her again."

"She seemed nice."

"You met her? You talked to her?"

"Was that wrong? She came into the room and told us all we didn't have to wait anymore and could collect our supplies for free."

"You talked to her personally?" Finn almost shouted at her.

"Rasa shrank back. "We didn't say much. What did I do wrong? I got permission. I said thank you. That's all."

"Did she ask you any questions?"

"Just the name of my ship."

Finn got up from the table. "We've got to go. Immediately. Come on, let's go."

"Actually, I intended to stay," Tina said. "There's still Evelle."

Finn stared at her, his nostrils flaring. Tina could see the thoughts whirling through his mind. He wiped sweat from his forehead.

Just what was he so afraid of?

Before she could ask, a clang sounded through the hull of the ship.

Tina got up from the table. "I better check what's happening."

She went outside the docking tube where it was indeed as Rasa had said: a couple of men in station overalls were setting up the power systems so that the ship could be recharged. No one asked for money. It was the strangest thing ever.

Not only that, they were doing the same to all the other ships in the passage. A great sense of excitement was in the air.

Tina went back inside, and explained what the sounds were from.

"I told you this would happen," Thor said.

Finn had already started bustling about, packing away items that would float through the cabin in flight.

"We need to decide what to do," Tina said. "I think some of us should stay here to find out where Evelle is, and if possible, to do whatever damage we can do to the pirates' illicit operations."

Finn gave her a concerned look. "Are you suggesting that you stay on the station alone?"

"Everyone who wants to stay, except perhaps you, because someone has to fly the craft, and it can't stay here when the docks are closed. Anyone who doesn't feel safe can go with the ship. Rasa should probably go with you."

Rasa said, "No way."

But Tina also didn't want to leave Finn alone with the ship. She thought she could trust him, but she was no longer certain. She was pretty sure he wouldn't defect to the pirates but wondered if he might panic and take off to Olympus without them.

"What am I supposed to do?" Rex asked.

"You're staying with me," Tina said. "I need you."

Rex glanced across the table at Rasa, an anguished look on his face. He asked, "What if they can't come back to the station?"

"The closure is not forever."

"It might be."

"Impossible. They still need to eat and, and they'll need all kinds of supplies that are only provided by commercial carriers."

"But Rasa has told the station director the name of the ship."

"Ship names are not secret. Anyone can look them up. I don't understand why giving out the ship name is significant."

"You don't know this woman," Finn said. "If she decides she doesn't like you, she will hound you to the edges of settled space. She doesn't forget. She has a team of people to act on her paranoia."

"It sounds like you know her," Rex said. "Is that something I missed?"

"Zia Partlow is his ex," Tina said.

Rex snorted. "This is like one of those stupid family dramas. If this is what being an adult is like, then I'm happy to stay a teenager."

Rasa laughed.

Tina said, "That would be funny if we weren't talking about two of the most powerful families in settled space. Look,

I don't know what the issue is either, but I know we can't trust the people in control of this station. We don't know if they're going to side with the pirates. But ultimately, they still need supplies and will need to open the docks and then you can come back."

"At which point they'll be waiting for the ship," Finn said.

Tina spread her hands. "Why? If they want us, they know we're here. They can just keep us here. We're vulnerable and we have been for the past few days. Why let us go and then wait for us to come back? It makes no sense."

Finn sighed and leaned forward with his elbows on his knees. "I just want to protect you from these people. They'll eat you up and spit you out."

"Rex and I will be fine. You leave and come back when the station reopens. We'll meet with Thor's friends to see if we can do anything about Evelle. We'll decide what to do after that when you come back here."

"What about the supplies?" Rasa asked.

"We get those now. If they're free, we grab as much as we can. Who knows when we'll next need to restock. For one, I'm sick of curry."

CHAPTER SIXTEEN

BEFORE GOING to collect their supplies, Tina wanted to wait until refuelling had finished. The departure permission Rasa had brought showed that they needed to pick up their supplies elsewhere at the docks, likely from a supply ship that had just arrived. Tina wondered if that was why the departure permits had been so delayed: because they were waiting for a ship to arrive.

She needed to know how she and Rex were going to survive after the ship left to wait near the station. Thor offered to put them up in a room, but Tina didn't want to put him and his son at risk. "We have some money now that we don't have to pay for refuelling. We can use temporary accommodation."

Thor wouldn't have any of it. "Take it from me: you don't want to stay there. Those guesthouses are not nice places."

"But I don't want to disturb your life either, and we've stayed at these places before. Who knows what trouble we'll get into once we find where the prisoners are? If they find out we stayed with you, you would get their attention, too."

"There is nothing in my life that they don't already know,

including that I have no love for pirates. They still need me to fix their stuff."

Tina enquired at the guest accommodation anyway, but it was full, besides ridiculously overpriced, so she had to accept Thor's offer.

Despite Rasa's casual remarks, Tina thought there was a bit more going on between her and Rex, and she was not terribly happy to stay on board the ship with Finn. But over the long and boring trip to Aurora, Rasa had developed quite a good knowledge of the operation of the ship, and she got along well with Finn. Besides, the geese would be staying on board and she would need to keep them from attacking Finn, who would be reluctant to feed them, seeing as they had developed such a strong dislike for him.

Rasa had been given a time slot in which they were allowed to visit the resupply area and they needed to find a trolley to carry their stuff.

Tina supervised the refuelling operations. The station staff responsible were professionals who had probably always worked here and now continued to perform their job as before.

Pirate rule or no pirate rule, ships still needed to be refuelled safely.

She made sure that Finn was up to speed with all the ship operations, but he had proven himself a capable pilot during the journey.

Tina and Rex had to make sure that they took all the tech devices and information they needed off the ship so that they could access them while staying with Thor. Maps and databases had to be copied.

Rex's harness computer had a huge capacity. Tina made copies of every imaginable bit of information that she thought might be of use, even stuff she thought they would never need. She asked Rex to break into and download as many maps and station databases as he could get, so he spent some time doing just that.

Jens helped him.

With the help of Jens, Rex could get into so many more places. Young as he was, Jens knew everything about the station's computer systems.

Meanwhile, Thor conjured up a couple of primitive radios for communicating with each other without using the official channels. "Mind you, once you start using these, it's my guess that they'll upset part of the station's communication channels and everyone in the station command room will be after you, so only use them in an emergency."

Once the *Alethia* left the docks, Finn was to keep the ship close enough to the station to remain in range of the radio.

Tina and Finn worked through several scenarios in which they lost contact, the ship was forced to move or couldn't come back to the station. Tina showed Finn all the manuals for midspace docking and how to adapt the docking tube for nonstandard vehicles. Many of these procedures she had never had to perform herself.

He listened and made notes.

This was what she liked in Finn. Having served in the military under the pressure of thousands of people dependent on his work, he was forced to consider every option in an unemotional way.

They made a long list of options and gave them priority numbers, so that in case communication failed, they would know which option either group was likely to have taken. They agreed that weapons was their weak point: they just didn't have many. Tina wasn't sure that carrying weapons in the station would be a good idea. She had the Fireseed she had confiscated at Kelso Station, but wasn't keen on having it on her while walking through the station. All stations had rules against carrying weapons. When a routine check revealed you had weapons, it led to an investigation, during which you might be held if the authorities thought it was warranted. So: no weapons, because she didn't want to run that risk.

The main priority would be to avoid situations where weapons would be necessary.

Meanwhile, the time slot for getting their supplies was approaching fast. They decided that everyone should go to get them except Finn, who really didn't want to enter the station. It was probably best that someone stay at the ship anyway, so Tina didn't mind. Thor and Jens insisted on coming, too, even though Tina said they could go home.

So she, Rex, Rasa, Thor and Jens went to collect the ship supplies. Tina had found a small trolley in the cargo hold, but doubted it would be big enough to carry everything they needed. They would probably have to make several trips.

The area surrounding the ship was a hive of activity, with station crews walking around, refuelling ships, and ship crew ferrying in supplies.

Tina and her companions followed the stream of people coming from a different area within the docks with crates of pre-packed rations and other essentials.

People were talking to each other in loud and happy voices, and a steady stream of people were coming down the hallway carrying all manner of things. They had electronics, furniture that someone had unbolted, and, strangely enough, sheets and blankets. On the corner of one of those, Tina spotted the insignia of the SF *Manila*.

"They're coming from the Federacy ship. They're looting it," Tina said.

Ahead, they came to an entry tube that was wide open, and seemed to be the source of all those people.

"This is where we're meant to get our supplies," Rasa said, looking at her map. "This" meaning the wide dock space where the *Manila* lay moored.

"You're kidding," Tina said.

"No, that's what it says on the instructions."

"That's right," Jens said. "Out of anything the pirates bring to the station, they never let any part go to waste."

Tina was horrified. "It looks like we can just go in."

She tried to spot if there were any guards posted, but there didn't seem to be any. The people walking in and out were just civilians, station residents and a mixture of seasoned merchants and irregular travellers. She even spotted young children going in.

"Let's go," Rasa said.

They followed the stream of people into the ship.

Tina struggled with feelings of sacrilege and betrayal. This was a secret ship. It was Evelle's home.

You never got to enter a Federacy fighter warship. Access was limited only to the crew. Even if you needed to travel on a troop carrier, and Tina had done that plenty of times, there were specific areas that were out of bounds, where sensitive equipment was housed.

It looked like this ship had been thrown completely open for anyone who wanted to come in.

Through the entry port, Tina, Rex, Rasa, Thor and Jens followed the stream through a maze of corridors, where people wandered around taking the crew's possessions from their bunks. She had no doubt that somewhere the pirates would be trying to get more valuable information out of the ship, but they seemed unashamed about looting it.

She wanted to know which cabin had been Evelle's, and wanted to protect her daughter's possessions from these strangers. Evelle might have kept mementoes like photographs. Maybe she'd kept in contact with her father.

All these thoughts made her feel sick.

A bit further down the hallway, the stream of people turned left and down a set of stairs in a central hallway where there were also lifts and screens displaying the status of the ship.

Big war ships functioned very differently from the *Alethia*. They took a long time to ramp up to be ready for departure. The *Alethia*'s ion drive was almost instantly ready. The *Manila*'s reactor needed to be carefully powered down when the ship came to dock, relying on the auxiliary engines for fine manoeuvring, and the reverse process happened when the ship departed. It took a number of days.

The departure readiness of the *Manila* showed seventy-five percent. That seemed a little on the high side.

The lower floor contained a massive galley kitchen with several workspaces, a serving window along one wall, and a supply storage area at the back.

Because this type of ship didn't have a rotating habitat, the workspaces were against the sides, facing each other. It was a strange sight, while standing on the floor. It was hard to imagine that kitchen staff would be working at both those ends. All the kitchen implements were held in place in knife blocks and spoon jars with magnets. A couple of dirty plates lay on the floor, evidence that the ship had been ambushed and the pirate attack had come suddenly.

Someone had opened the banks of storage cupboards at

the back and had taken out all the crew rations that were stored in closed crates. The lids lay on the floor and people were rummaging through them, picking out the ones they liked.

Rex groaned. "Not more curry, please."

His eyes were better than Tina's, and when she bent over the opened crates, she saw that he was right.

"Curry it is, then."

With all the people scavenging the supplies, the crates emptied quickly. It was like shark feeding.

She and Rex started filling up the baskets on the trolley before everything was gone, while Thor held the trolley steady and Jens disappeared into the door to the storage area.

He came back with an arm full of packets. "This might be better."

He dumped the parcels in the top basket.

It was. These parcels were much more varied, and many contained single items, not complete meals.

There were even luxuries like bread and real meat, all wrapped up in preserving parcels.

"That must be the officer meals," Tina said.

It was everyone for themselves. There was no control about who took what for how many.

It was sickening and, at the same time, the reality was that they had to take part.

"Let's take as much as we can put in the trolley," she said. "We're going to need to come back to get more, but this will be a good start. Pack it in as efficiently as you can."

They proceeded to stuff the trolley full of rations, and then someone found some laundry bags and they filled those up, too.

One bag got so big that Rasa couldn't carry it any more, so

Rex took some of the content out, put it in the second bag and then filled it up so that he could carry two bags while Tina and Rasa each carried one and Thor wheeled the trolley.

So burdened, they returned to the *Alethia*. They emptied their loot, folded up the bags and returned to the *Manila*.

They filled up their bags again, and took the contents back to their own ship.

Inside the cabin, Finn had laid out all the previous rations according to their contents.

He said, "I don't like curry. Why did you get so much curry?"

"Most of what they had was curry. It's better than nothing," Tina said.

But even as she said that, she could smell the curry and see the yellow glop with unidentifiable chunks in a bowl.

"We probably have enough to get us to Olympus, but I'd like to go for another trip," Tina said. "Just in case we strike misfortune, because I don't want to be stuck and have to visit one of the stations again." In her mind she thought not so much about detours, but about having an extra passenger on board, and maybe Evelle would bring a friend, too.

They needed to plan for everything.

Then they went back to the *Manila*, where the stream of people going in and out was even bigger.

Word must have gotten around in the station that there was something to be had, because not all of the people were ship crew.

In most communities, even Gandama, looting was a crime. Nobody seemed to care here.

"Isn't that what pirates do?" Rex said when she told him about it.

"I wonder what they do when they start looting from each

other," Tina said. "It's all very well looting from someone you don't know, from a society that's not yours, but once people start taking each other's possessions, that's when it becomes troublesome."

"Maybe that's why everyone is so suspicious."

They went down the stairs into the landing that led to the galley. The big screen display showed the ship at seventy-seven percent readiness. She swore last time it said seventy-five. So the ship was being prepared for departure? Even while it was being looted. What were the pirates going to do with it?

CHAPTER SEVENTEEN

THEY FILLED up the trolley for the last time. Still more people streamed into the galley. The crates with rations had long been emptied, and people were now scavenging parcels from the sections that couldn't be removed.

Others were opening whichever cupboards along the sides of the galley walls they could reach, climbing on each other's shoulders if necessary, and handing down storage boxes and drawers. They collected plates, and cups and cutlery. They argued with each other over which side of the kitchen was theirs.

"Are we all done?" Tina asked. She didn't like how the atmosphere was turning aggressive in the galley. By now, most of the ship crew was gone, and the people rummaging through the cupboards were pirates. Arguments broke out over certain items. Most of them spoke various dialects that Tina didn't understand. Men and women in different dress codes worked together. A group in dark red appeared to be a family, a grandfather, a father, a mother and two teenage daughters. All of them pirates, but unarmed, and interested only in pots and pans. The grandfather was guarding a hoard of them, shooing away a young boy in blue clothing who tried to sneak off with one of the pans.

Those groups were the real Freerangers, from the tight-knit, highly independent shipworlds, and they appeared to be different from the other ship crews in that they looked for items to sell.

A mutant pirate with grey skin and a toad-like appearance came to the door and looked in. The grandfather clamped his jaw and glared at the man.

That was an interesting exchange. Artan, Jackson Hirsch, wasn't born a pirate. Tina didn't know how he came to be a pirate, but she hadn't given much thought to the possibility that the "real" Freeranger pirates didn't like him at all.

The toad-pirate remained at the door, returning the grandfather's angry stare.

The Freeranger mother in dark red called both her daughters, and the group sidled out the door, leaving behind a number of pots they couldn't carry.

The boy in blue ran to grab them, but another boy had noticed them, and a fight broke out. The blue mother yelled at the other boy, and his family yelled back. In particular a young man got very angry, and came at the blue mother. He grabbed her by the arm, and for one moment looked like he was going to attack her.

"Oy. Stop that," Tina called out.

It was a reaction that bubbled up out of her memory, where she used to tell off younger workers at Project Charon to keep them from getting into worse problems and facing disciplinary action if they were caught in a fistfight.

She might be much older now, but her voice had lost none of its authority.

The boy let go of the mother's arm and went back to his family. The blue family eyed Tina. A man who looked like the father of the family gave a tiny nod.

"Let's get out of here," Tina said. She had no intention of getting involved in pirate politics.

Thor wheeled the trolley to the landing, where many people burdened with loot waited for the lifts.

The tone of conversations around them was angry.

Two toad-pirate guards stood on the stairs. The bank of screens played clips of oddly peaceful scenery. The ship's readiness had climbed to seventy-eight percent.

The lift door opened, and the waiting crowd surged forward. Tina, Rex, Rasa, Jens and Thor were caught up, especially the latter because he held the trolley, he couldn't see, he wanted nothing to fall off and he could only go where people pushed him.

They managed to fit into the lift.

It complained about being overloaded and two people had to get off before it would move.

If Tina had hoped that the upstairs landing would be less busy, she was wrong. Coming out of the lift, they were met with a cordon of toad-pirates.

Many people streamed down the stairs, some of them pushing, others running and half-climbing over the railing. Most of those people were Freeranger pirates.

Screens around the lifts and stairwell showed different parts of the ship, most of them also crowded, except one: the ship's bridge was abandoned.

Using the trolley as snowplough, Tina guided Thor into the passage that led back to the entry tube.

They were not the only group trying to get out. They formed a conga line of ship crews inching through what appeared to be a series of arguments between pirates, who were yelling from both sides of the passage, over the heads of those trying to get out of the ship.

But around the corner, they ran into trouble. The passage was blocked. A great mass of people was waiting to get through to the entrance tube of the ship.

Tina looked at Rex. "Can you see what's going on?"

He looked over the heads of the crowd. "One of those warty pirate guys is out the front," he said.

"What is he doing?"

"He's yelling something."

Yes, Tina could hear a man shouting, but the words were unintelligible.

She tried to stand on her toes to see. Rex couldn't flip out the step on the side of his harness, because his hands were full with bags of rations.

A few other people shouted, followed by a clang that reverberated through the floor under Tina's feet.

Thor swore. "You don't discharge weapons inside a ship or station."

People screamed.

The crowd surged back. Tina grabbed Rasa's arm and pulled her behind the trolley as someone tripped over the wheels, and other people tripped over the man who had fallen. Other people clambered over the top.

Thor said, "Come on! Take cover behind the trolley."

Jens and Rasa crouched in the shelter. Tina helped Thor to keep the trolley in place. People were bumping it and tripping over the wheels and pushing it aside.

They wouldn't be able to hold their position for long.

The back of the trolley already pushed into Tina's legs. If

she lost control over it, the crowd would trample Jens, Thor and Rasa.

"Wait."

With a great athletic jump, Rex vaulted over the trolley. He put his back against the wall and simply pushed people away from the trolley. He was formidable. No one got past him. Tina helped shelter Rasa and Jens, and she and Thor made sure the trolley didn't move.

Then the main bulk of the crowd was gone, and the devastation became clear. The wall of the hall that gave access to the ship's entrance tube, was blackened, and part of the wall panel had melted, exposing the electronics within.

The normally spotless floor was covered in smudges of blood and a couple of discarded items of clothing. There was even a young man slumped against the wall, blood running from a gash in his forehead into his eye. A couple of people from a pirate Freeranger family stood around him, attempting to get him up.

A woman, presumably the boy's mother, was yelling at the pirate guards. They spoke a strong Sinolese dialect that Tina didn't understand, but her words cut into her heart. These were real Freerangers, people who were happy simply to scavenge deep space for items they could sell including structures and items abandoned by settlers. They had made their living like this for generations. Artan was an intruder to them. He might have infiltrated pirate society, but their behaviour made it clear that they had no love for him or his warty-faced friends.

Ahead, at the entry to the access tube, stood a handful of warty men. Their skin was grey, the jawbones lined by tentacles that were slowly moving. Their hands also had long tentacles with which they held onto their weapons. One of the men had extended those tentacles and used them to scour the ground like skinny worms. Each of these tentacles probed the ground before returning to a dark spot on the pirate's arm. Were they tasting the ground for scents left by the people who had been present at the fight?

Two men who looked like they came from a merchant ship approached Tina and her group from behind. They walked past, ignored the pirate with the tentacles and marched up to the door.

The guards let them past.

Tina seized the opportunity and followed them. "We're just merchants," she said to the pirate. He gave her a blank look with a beady eye. Tina wasn't even sure he understood her. But he let them walk past unhindered. Tina's heart was thudding. That could easily have ended differently.

Tina checked that everyone was all right, which they were. Rasa had a bruise from where the trolley had been pushed into her leg and Jens had acquired some scratches on his left arm from being pushed by the crowd. Rex inspected the legs and arms of his harness.

"You sook. It's made to be scratch-resistant," Tina said. "Help us get out of here."

The four of them hurried through the passages and reached the ship not much later.

Finn came to the door, his face concerned.

"I'm glad you're back. You took so long. There was a lot of noise in the station."

"Well, that's where we've come from." She told him about the brutal fight in the ship and how the pirates from the ship-worlds didn't seem to like the warted pirates.

"We won't be going back for supplies any more. We need to

concentrate on the next stage now. Once everything is completed, you should leave as soon as possible."

"Are you still sure about this?" Finn asked. "You don't have to stay. It seems like there will be trouble."

"I don't have to? Do you have a daughter? No?"

He raised his hands. "All right, I get it."

"No, you don't get it. Don't tell me what I should do. She's been captured by pirates. We might not have the best mother-daughter relationship in all the settled worlds, but don't tell me that I don't have to do something for her if I can. I'm not going to die knowing that I could have done something to save her. Everyone else can go with the ship, but I'm staying here and sticking to the plan."

CHAPTER EIGHTEEN

IT WAS TIME TO GO.

Tina and Rex collected their bags. Tucked away in Tina's bag, wrapped in her jacket, was the Fireseed she had confiscated at Kelso Station. She had debated leaving the weapon on board, but Finn said it definitely wasn't any use to him.

Tina kept an eye on Rex. He kept looking at Rasa, but neither of them gave any indication that they would find the separation difficult. She did detect a small twitch in Rasa's face, but that could be because she had an itchy nose.

It was difficult to figure out what was going on between those two.

Tina checked whether the radio Thor had made worked, got the thumbs-up from Finn, and left the craft with Thor, Jens and Rex.

It felt strange to leave her most important possession behind with someone else.

Rasa closed the door of the craft, and Finn set in motion the process to disconnect from the station. The ship showed full readiness. The station's airlock door slid shut. A line of lights blinked red on the control panel. The display underneath said, "Careful. Do not attempt to open this door."

A screen next to the access tube displayed a feed from an outside camera, showing a piece of the station and part of the ship.

Tina wanted to watch until the two decoupled, but they had better get going, because people might get suspicious. After all she was not supposed to be at the station once the ship left.

All around, people were leaving, and at the end of the passage, some people were coming in their direction with barriers. The docks were being closed, as Thor had said.

They walked quickly with Jens and Thor through the passages.

A number of other people were also going in their direction. They were mostly dockworkers, people in overalls with tools or trolleys.

They went through the hall with the lifts where she had seen Evelle. A lot of warty pirates hung around, keeping the station workers away from the lifts. Had they captured even more ships? Were they bringing in other prisoners?

The lift door opened, but the lift was empty. Two of the warty pirates went in.

Other pirates moved barriers forward once the last of the civilians had come out of the docking areas.

Tina, Rex, Thor and Jens walked through the station, not speaking much other than some chat about shops and other unimportant things, like life at Cayelle.

They arrived at Thor and Jens' apartment.

"Why don't you show the guests where they can sleep," Thor said, walking into the living room.

Jens showed Tina and Rex a room that was fully fitted out

to have visitors, with two beds, a small cupboard and two chairs. It was small, but comfortable enough.

"Do you often have visitors?" Tina said.

"People come to visit every now and then, when they want their equipment to be fixed. Not too much any more."

"Do people travel from elsewhere to have their equipment fixed?"

"Miners," Jens said. "It's specialised equipment."

Tina set her bag on the chair and took off her boots. At Gandama she walked barefoot a lot of the time. She didn't like wearing shoes indoors.

While they had been in the bedroom, Thor had started to prepare dinner.

It was amazing to watch him, because he knew where everything stood in the kitchen. Watching him, you would never be able to tell he was blind.

He said without looking over his shoulder, "Sit down, I'll make you some tea."

"I'll help, if you tell me what I can do," Tina said.

"That's not necessary. It's a simple thing, and there's not much space in here."

So Tina sat down at the table, feeling awkward. She didn't feel like making chitchat and was bad at it anyway.

"If I want to look for my daughter, where should I start?"

"We'll need proper maps."

"Rex has already discovered some maps."

"We'll have a look. We've probably seen those maps before, but they're all a little bit different, and each one teaches us something we didn't yet know."

"You've made a study of this before? You say 'us' and 'we'. Does that mean there are more of you?"

"You'll see." He didn't elaborate further.

With his quiet manner, he reminded her somewhat of Dexter, who always responded to her irritation about him not telling her things with "You didn't ask," or "If they don't talk about it, they don't need to know."

Even Finn was like that. Heavens, why did she always manage to seek out the men who had to be requested expressly, in triplicate and in writing if possible, to talk about things that *normal* people would talk about freely?

Dinner was done, and they started eating, while Rex and Jens filled the awkward space by talking about Gandama. Jens seemed impressed that Rex was able to run the shop by himself, and was even more impressed when Rex showed him pictures of his old harness.

"You used to wear that?"

"It was the best we could get at the time," Tina said. "It's very hard to get things in Gandama. Not many people live there, and transport is very expensive."

Thor snorted. "Which is why I never went to a planet. There is less of everything there, and it costs twice as much."

"Except fresh air and plants and animals."

"I've seen enough of that stuff with those birds of yours," Thor said.

Tina couldn't imagine how someone couldn't want to see blue sky and waving fields of grain. All of a sudden she was back in her youth in Tirkala where she would sit on the veranda looking over the fields. She and her friends would catch lizards under the planks of the veranda. Even back then, she was always growing and keeping things.

Her family had been surprised when she signed up for the Force, but joining the military was not the reason. She joined because the military paid for her studies, and they needed biologists.

"So how did you even start the shop?" Jens wanted to know. "Is it hard?"

He seemed keen to go to a planet. Maybe that was his attraction to Rex: the very thing that Rex wanted to escape from.

"I saw an opportunity. There were a lot of empty buildings, and people were talking about putting a lot of houses in the area, and I figured that people would need surveillance equipment, because that's what they usually do in a new development, where some other people don't take the law very seriously."

"But how did you learn about all these things?"

And then Tina told them how she had to learn all of it herself, mostly from old manuals that she pilfered from second-hand stores and obscure databases, and that the shop did very well, because no one in Gandama had sold anything like that before.

Then the discussion turned to the cactuses.

"Seriously, they move? Are these animals or plants?" Thor wanted to know.

"I still think they're plants. They're not very smart, and they react to light and darkness."

"That sounds very much like something you've seen, Jens."

It sounded like a prompt for Jens to start talking, but Jens was looking at his hands. He let a very long pause go by.

Then he said, "I was really stupid."

"Come on son, tell them the story."

Jens looked down at his knees. Eventually, he started talking.

"I was with some of my mates, and we were just having fun. Nothing unusual, nothing that any kid wouldn't do. It was just after the occupation by the pirates, and we were being let back into the station after having been shut up in our apartments for quite a long time. We were bored and looking for something to do. We had this kid in our group who always wanted to explore. He would climb into things and see where they led. We were always joking how one day he would open the door to an airlock and would be sucked into space."

Then he sat in thought for a bit.

"You don't have to tell us if it's hard to talk about," Tina said.

Jens shook his head. "It's important. It's just that..." A visible shudder went through him.

"Anyway, we were bored, and the kid said he had discovered this passage that would take us right into the pirate headquarters. At the time, there were all kinds of rumours going around about what they did to women, and some people said that they had a lab where they cut off the flaps on their skin, and grew them into creatures. No one had ever seen these creatures, and I have no idea how that rumour started, except that some of the pirates would sometimes walk around with bandages, and we wondered what they were for.

"Anyway, we got into this passage, which was a maintenance passage that we had used before. I knew it, because it leads all the way around the station, with lots of little side passages to secret storage areas and control rooms that are used by maintenance staff. It also has exits to the normal habitat areas. It's just a second network of corridors that can be closed off in case there is an emergency, with rooms where people can shelter or hide. It's like an inner shell of the station."

"And no one lives there?" Tina asked.

"It's not very big, and wouldn't house all the people permanently, but it's a place where people can survive for a little while in case of a disaster."

That was an interesting approach. Most of the stations functioned with segments that had doors that could be closed hermetically.

Jens continued, "So the pirates took possession of the station, but they weren't terribly interested in us. Many people left the station after the occupation. The pirates didn't stop them. In fact, as you've already seen, they encourage people to leave in big waves."

Tina said, "I'm guessing this goes hand-in-hand with the capture of a ship that carries enough supplies to resupply all the ships that are waiting to leave."

"You got it," Thor said. He nodded to his son. The difficult part of the story was yet to come.

"So we got into these corridors, and we walked for a really long time. Of course I know it only felt like a long time because we were in a narrow corridor, with very little light and no people and no doors, and every moment you wonder whether you're going to blunder into something that you're not supposed to see. So it feels like you're in there forever because it's scary and dark. And then we got to this stairwell and we went down two or three flights of stairs, I don't remember. There was a door at the bottom of the stairs, and we opened it."

He let another silence go past. He had clamped his hands on his knees, his knuckles white.

"The room was full of people," he said. And again he said nothing for a while.

"I guess these were not happy people?" Tina said.

Jens shook his head. "I don't know if they were alive or dead. They were in these large tubes with blue light inside. I didn't want to get any closer. Some of them didn't look like people any more, because they had so many growths on their skin that they looked like giant walking plants. Like those cactuses you were talking about."

He paused for another while.

"Anyway, my friend, his name was Marcus, went looking around, showing me all these frozen people covered in mush-rooms or something, and then all of a sudden, these beefy mutant guys turned up. We tried to run away, but they caught Marcus. I tried to free him, but these were big guys, and they were using tentacles on their arms to hold him down. He was screaming, but there was nothing I could do. He pleaded with me to leave him, and to run to find help. The last I saw of him, they were forcing him into one of those cylinders. We ran back to the passage, and escaped as quickly as we could. I've never heard from Marcus again. They probably froze him. None of us have been the same since. Every time I see those warty pirates, I see that big room. One of the others in the group, he was just a kid, killed himself by walking out of the airlock. It made him crazy."

"Wait, they actually produce people like that on purpose?" Tina asked.

Thor nodded. "There have been rumours, but no one had seen it."

"Why?"

"They are very strong, and people say that the modified people live a very long time."

Tina had also heard that. "But then to live looking like that wouldn't be much fun."

"That wouldn't make a difference if you're a pirate," Thor said.

"You know, I don't think they're true pirates."

Thor shrugged. "Pirates, Freerangers, whatever they want to call themselves."

"No, I think the Freerangers are different. They are the original pirates, the people who live in shipworlds and live off retrieving and selling discarded space junk. They're not toad people. Do you know where this room was?" Tina asked Jens. "Would you be able to find your way back to it?"

"I would, but I'd be very surprised if that door was still open," Jens said.

And then Tina had a more chilling thought. If this was where they produced new pirate soldiers, then maybe that was what they were doing to the crew of the Federacy warship.

"Do you know how long this process takes?" she asked. She felt sick.

"I know nothing about it," Thor said.

"I don't want to know anything about it," Jens said.

Then another thought. "Do you think that the people in the station who've gone missing are also there? That they're trying to build a giant army of horrible people who are barely still human to destroy all of us?"

Thor shrugged. "Who knows?"

But the implication was there. It was just too horrible to contemplate.

Yes, Tina had noticed how these infected people had increased in number and were popping up everywhere, but— "I assumed it was an infection."

"It may be, but it's not an infection that is passed from one person to the other easily. You have to have serious contact with whatever it is that causes the infection. I have a friend who you'll meet later who's a scientist. He can tell you more about it."

So it was an infection that the pirates under Artan were

deliberately spreading. And she and Rex had value, because despite having had exposure to it, they were resistant. They were important, not as a defence against the infection, but as a weapon against the pirates. And the pirates wanted her and Rex because they wanted to keep anyone from having that power over them.

That was the theory, at least. Finn was right: a lot of people wanted to profit from her genetics and her information.

She was tired, and was about to propose that she and Rex turn in early so that they could start on their plans tomorrow, but then there was a knock on the door. Jens went to open it.

Three people came in, two women and a tall man with greying hair and a short beard.

Tina recognised him immediately. She gasped. "Vasily."

He frowned, his expression blank. "Have we met before?"

She studied his face, and noticed slight differences from the man she thought she recognised who had sent her a message before he said he'd die.

"Sorry, I thought you were someone else. You look a lot like someone I haven't seen for a long time."

"Vasily Dimitrov."

"Yes. Do you know him?"

"I did. He's missing, presumed dead. He was my twin brother." He held out his hand. "I'm Arkady."

Tina shook it. "Tina Freeman."

"I figured as much."

"I got your brother's message," Tina said. "Eventually, even if I got it fifteen years late."

CHAPTER NINETEEN

ARKADY INTRODUCED the two women who were with him as prominent ex-scientists for the Federacy, both from Olympus. They'd been travelling when they became stuck on Aurora because of pirate action. Jetta Bengtson was a physicist in middle age with a severe bun of greying blond hair. Yalinda Singh was younger and had worked in the medical labs.

Tina had heard of Jetta, but didn't know Yalinda. Both women already knew who Tina was, from Arkady's stories.

Jetta explained to Tina that the group associated with Thor consisted of scientists and technicians. "We've all gotten together because we realise we can't beat this thing alone. It's been hard enough to retrieve available data from the remnants of Project Charon. Some of it was highly classified. These are the conclusions we've drawn from materials we've obtained: there are two reactions from people to the rift infection. The first is the route taken by the Federacy: if no one is allowed to mention it, write papers on it and share it with other scientists, they assume that the material will dissipate into space and no one will ever encounter it in high enough concentrations to do any harm. Never mind we still don't know what triggers an infection. The other type of people see the unlimited genetic potential of this material, and they want to use the material, and make money from selling it. We already see rumours spreading through the settled worlds that an infection will make you invincible and will make you live longer."

"Is that not true, then?" Tina asked. Thor had said so.

"From what we've seen, it may be true, but it comes at a very high cost."

"That you look like a toad."

"That people who are infected change because the infection spreads to their organs. It changes the way people behave. It turns them into something else, no longer human. We can't allow this to spread, especially when it's being touted as a cure for major diseases and people are making money from it. But if we speak out, our jobs will be terminated, like yours."

"So, you're a kind of resistance?"

"If you want to call it that. We try to be very quiet about it, though. It's dangerous to speak out."

They sat down around the table, and Thor busied himself making more tea.

The women told their stories, of how, after their travel to Olympus was no longer possible, they'd been part of the station's staff and had managed to escape the fate that had befallen so many of them.

Jetta had been sick on the day the pirates occupied the station, but all her colleagues were missing. Yalinda had worked for a private lab that hadn't been affected because it was a private business in a different part of the station, but a few days after the pirates invaded, they raided the lab, smashed all the equipment and made sure that no one had the resources to return to work.

"We've been struggling to make ends meet," she said. "My parents relied on my income, and my father has had to go back to work. It's a disgrace that he has to work for the pirates."

Tina felt tired, and hoped she was listening properly to everything they said. This was too important to allow herself to doze off.

She said to Arkady, "Do you know what happened to your brother?"

"If you received his message, you're probably the last person to have heard from him."

"There was some information in his letter, but not much about where he was and what had happened. He said he might be dead, but it's been sitting in the document box for such a long time that I have no idea what happened since."

"We last had contact with him at about the same time. We only received a vague farewell letter. He said he didn't want to say where he was for fear of exposing people who were with him who might still be able to escape to safety. We've done some work, and have revealed that he was somewhere near Project Charon when he sent the message. We think he was either already captured or soon to be captured by pirates."

"Did you work for the Federacy as well?" Tina asked.

"No. My brother and I both had the same training, but I chose to go for the big money and started working for private enterprises. That's where I first found out about the effort by pirates to buy up samples and knowledge about this strange rift material. I warned my brother because I knew he was working on it at the time, and we grew concerned about the things we were seeing, that people were using it to deliberately infect living organisms, like plants."

"I saw that when I worked at the project. There might have been some internal papers about it."

"When was this?"

"It must have been close on twenty years ago. I was working for the project at the time. Why didn't your brother contact me then? It would have been much easier because we were working in the same place."

"You were considered too much of a risk. Dexter was known to be sympathetic to commercial interests. He was frustrated that the full potential of the rift material was not being used. He said that if the Federacy wasn't going to do anything with it, people would come in and steal it and do illegal things."

"How ironic."

"Anyway, you were not in our sights. You were also having lots of trouble with your daughter at the time, so we didn't think that you would have any interest in being in the scientific ethics society."

Tina had heard of this society, and she remembered a number of people going to talks and meetings after work. She'd gone to a couple of talks. And yes, she had wondered why she'd never been invited to become a member, but Evelle was also giving her grief back then, and if she'd been invited, she would have declined anyway. "Hang on, are you saying that this society is the resistance? The group I knew about just organised talks. I didn't have time to attend many of them, because of all the things I was going through at the time, but I did go to some."

"That's what we used to call ourselves. We did talk about a whole lot of things other than ethics, but it was a way to disguise our concerns from those who might care. People expect scientists to debate things, so no one thought anything of it. We scoped out possible members of a more secret group at the meetings, judging by the opinions they displayed."

"Is that what you're doing now? Banding together with scientists to beat the pirates?"

"I don't know that we're powerful enough to defeat the pirates. We have grown much bigger and include a lot more people. We've started giving so-called education lessons to tell people what is happening. We don't talk about the pirates or about station management or anything political, so we can fly under the radar."

"How many people are we talking about?"

"On the station, probably about two thousand."

"Two thousand, out of how many? The station is said to have a population of a million."

"That was before the occupation. At the moment, it's much less. And I'm only talking about two thousand people who are members of our organisation and who regularly come to gatherings. I'm not talking about their sympathisers, or their families. If we take all those people into consideration, the numbers are going to be much greater. Especially if we become more active."

"So, how many people are there on the station at the moment?"

"Bearing in mind that we aren't privileged to look into the station operation databases, we guess probably about three hundred thousand."

"That's just the public side of the station?"

"Yes. A great number of people disappeared during and shortly after the occupation. We simply don't know where they went. Others left, but this is a small proportion, because many people were long-term residents who didn't have the means to leave."

"And you've found no indication of what happened to the people who disappeared?"

"Other than that we suspect there are still a lot of people in the restricted side of the station, no. We don't know if they're the missing people. We don't know if they're different people. The heat might not be generated by people at all. We know that a lot of ships arrive and depart when they close the docks to the public. The problem is motivating the people to do something. Our evidence isn't strong enough. People are scared. People are complacent. They get on with their lives."

"People are stupid and careless," Thor said. His voice was dark. "They pretend that the occupation is the new normal and carry on with their pitiful daily lives."

"You're saying that people have been happy with the occupation?"

At the same time Thor was about to say something angry, Arkady continued, "I wouldn't say happy."

Thor snorted. "They are happy, though, because they occasionally get free things, and the pirates leave them alone for the most part. There is less control and people often like that, even if it also leads to bad things."

Arkady said, "You have to understand this. Prior to the occupation, the station management went through a long period of political turmoil that made people switch off, and occasionally made them angry about the lack of morals of their leaders. Mostly the people stopped caring; they only wanted the politics and the scandals and the corruption to go away. And strangely enough, when the pirates came in and made station management irrelevant, most people were happy to see the worst offenders go, and didn't care terribly much about what happened to them. They were glad that the political circus stopped and they could go on with their daily lives without having to put up with the antics of corrupt politicians."

"That sounds somewhat familiar," Tina said.

"Have you heard about it?"

"No, but it is the story of the downfall of so many human civilisations. Somebody stopped caring and so the bad guys got in, and humanity spent the next couple of decades figuring out how anyone ever allowed it to happen."

He nodded.

"Anyway, we're hoping that if we can show them what happened to the people who went missing and the station residents get angry, we can turn them into a great force."

"You're an incurable optimist," Thor said.

"I don't think so. Up to now, there have been many rumours, but because they are just rumours there can't be any anger behind them. Few people have been able to make the link between some of the strange activities that go on in the docks, when the pirates close the station to all arrivals, and their vanished love ones."

"So were you based on Aurora Station when the pirates occupied it?" Tina asked Arkady.

"No, I wasn't. I came in after I heard about this from my friend here." He looked at Jetta. "And she was able to let me know what had happened by pure chance, because she was not at work that day."

Tina asked, "Are you planning to do anything?"

Jetta said, "We have to start somewhere fighting this madness. We have to find a flashpoint for people to get concerned about the pirate movement. We have to get the Federacy Assembly to take us seriously before it is too late and our Armed Forces have been depleted too much to do anything."

"It looks that way already," Tina said.

Jetta agreed. "The Federacy still call it quelling an uprising.

They still talk about the pirates as if they are poorly organised rogues, family groups living in shipworlds."

"There are still those," Tina said. "To be honest, I don't think they get along with Artan any better than we do."

"The point is, the Federacy on far away Olympus still don't understand what is happening here. Maybe some of them do, but they think the problem will go away by itself."

"Surely they'll hear about the capture of a Federacy warship."

"Maybe. The pirates have captured smaller vessels before with no consequences."

"This is a Star Fighter."

"I know."

"They were allowing people to loot the ship. We went in because we were told to get our supplies there. It was sickening."

"That's what usually happens. Supplies in the station are rather short, so under the pretence of continuing normal commercial operations, they allow ships to come in to conduct small trades. But there are not enough supplies on the station to restock the ships, so whenever a large vessel is captured, they allow all the small ship crew to plunder the ship."

"This is a Federacy warship. One of the most secretive ships of humanity. I worked for the Federacy for many years, and never set foot on one of them. Either these pirates don't know what they have, or they're completely stupid."

"They're not. They know very well the treasure trove of information they'll find here. Artan knows what he's got. He will have posted his men to stop people taking anything of importance from the ship, like anything from the engine or the bridge. I am guessing, going by previous occasions, that some shipworld people were trying to get into one of these places and they were stopped and this is how the fights today broke out."

It could well be. Tina hadn't seen how it happened.

She brought the discussion back to the reason she had stayed behind. "Do you have any idea where the crew of the Star Fighter would be?"

"Oh, I wouldn't hold out too much hope for them. Likely they never made it off the ship."

"They did. I saw them being led away."

Arkady took in a whistling breath. "Artan must have plans for them, then. Maybe he needs them to operate the ship."

"When we were inside the ship, it was ramping up for departure."

He frowned at her, and Thor said, "Are you sure? I didn't notice anything. Normally, when the big ships fire up, the floor vibrates in a very soft way that most people wouldn't notice. I didn't feel that."

"The readiness indicator was going up. At least according to the screen in the stairwell."

"I saw that, too," Jens said.

"Hmmm," Thor said.

"Maybe the software running the display was faulty," Arkady said.

"Could be," Tina said. "Although it's my experience that if a military ship says it's ramping up for departure, it really is ramping up for departure. They have too much duplication on board to be dependent on one faulty routine."

"True," Thor said. "I agree."

"So why is the ship ramping up for departure without the crew?" Arkady asked. "Maybe the crew are being kept at close quarters and they have defected—"

"Never."

"I understand you were in the military, but—"

"Never," Tina said again.

"How can you be so sure of—"

"That crew contains my daughter. She is the meanest military hard-faced bitch you've met in your life. She would not hand herself over to a bunch of toadfaces. I saw her. She had not defected, and nor had any of the other crewmembers. Those highly specialised people on board these Star Fighters would not do that."

"Whoa, calm down. I was just speculating."

"The crew are on the station. They're not in the ship. They're alive. I think Artan wants or needs them for something. I think they're held prisoner somewhere in the station. The reason I'm here is that I am going to free my daughter."

"That is a very big and dangerous task."

"It's why I'm still here and why I didn't leave with my ship that's hanging around somewhere waiting for the docks to reopen. I am going to free her. Tell me what my best chances are and what I need to do to get into wherever she might be."

She'd had enough of talk and speculation. It was time to do something.

CHAPTER TWENTY

THE FIRST TASK was to get accurate plans of the restricted part of the station. Arkady said that he'd share with Tina whatever they had, even though he thought her mission to free Evelle was reckless and too dangerous.

The group had been collecting a lot of data on the station's metrics, which included heat maps, the use of energy and the number of flights coming in and going out, especially during periods of official closure of the docks.

Arkady explained that one of their members used to work in station operations and could calculate how many people were likely to live in the other half of the station based on their use of power and other vitals, like oxygen. Tina asked so many questions that Arkady ended up contacting the man and asking him to come to Thor's apartment.

His name was Matt. He was very slim and short for a man, and he arrived wearing baby-blue polka-dotted pyjamas. Yes, it was late. When Tina raised her eyebrows at his attire, he said, "My daughter's. She's out there somewhere. She's a teacher. We have to keep believing."

It was precisely those sections—the schools, the administrative offices, the hospital—that were in the sector of the station that the pirates had confiscated. Matt had escaped capture because he was working a night shift on the day of the occupation.

He detailed with great precision where the greatest concentrations of people were and where their communication hub and command centres were likely to be.

Tina asked about the room with the frozen people that Jens had told her about.

"Oh yes, that's very likely to be here." He spun his projected model in the air and pointed at a section that was darker. "We call this the cold zone. There is little human activity here. The agriculture plant is in this section as well. I don't know about this room that young Jens has talked about. I don't disbelieve him, but my data simply doesn't show me anything about it, because there is little human activity."

"And the command centre is here?" Tina pointed at the model. "And this area around it has a high population?"

"As far as we can track, yes."

Tina was reminded of what she loved about being a scientist: separating truth from hype, fact from rumour and, sometimes, whupping the backsides of rumour-mongering politicians with hard data. Never piss off a scientist, the saying went. They were likely to hit back with a list of your little lies and misbehaviour dating back twenty years.

Damn, she loved and missed people like Matt.

She said, "This cold zone is on the other side of the docks. If we could get in, we could walk through this sector into the more densely populated area."

"You could, or you could not, depending on how the entrances are guarded."

"My guess: not terribly well. I know a bit about security. I haven't been impressed with what I've seen. I think Artan and his mates are too busy with whatever they're doing to expect any action from the station's population. I think, on the whole, they're probably right, but that doesn't mean we can't sneak in."

Thor said, "You could absolutely do this, if you pretend you're maintenance crew."

"It's too dangerous," Arkady said. "If you were caught, you would endanger all the work we've done so far."

Thor said, "What's the point of having the information if you're not going to use it?"

"We're too few."

Tina said, "Look, you don't have to send anyone with us. You don't even have to give us anything. We'll study the information you have, but won't take any of it that they can use to track back to you. This is my operation. You can help, or you can stay in the safety of your apartments. I'm going."

Not much later, the two women and Matt left, but Arkady stayed behind.

He said, "Look, I'm sorry. I know this is not what you wanted."

"I would have expected a bit more support."

"These people are scared. It's not like they've never tried anything, but they're scientists, not fighters, and many have lost friends and family members even after the occupation."

"It's all right. You don't have to defend them."

"But I do, because I feel responsible for giving you hope."

"I never had that much to begin with. But I am going to try this. Because that's what you do for your family."

"Yeah." He looked at his hands. "I wish I could still do that for mine."

"You really have no idea what happened to your brother?" Tina asked.

"We haven't heard from him, other than that message that he was probably going to be dead by the time we got it."

"But he might have survived. He would have been far too valuable for the pirates just to kill him."

"Oh, he would have realised that. He wouldn't have let the pirates get their hands on him."

Tina realised that this was precisely what Vasily would have done. "I am so sorry for your loss."

He nodded, and they were silent for a while.

"One thing no one really understands," Tina said, "is the mechanism by which this infection, if you can call it that, spreads from person to person—when it's not done deliberately, at least. I feel there is a story to be told there. It has something to do with a rapid-growth stage in the life-cycle called 'bloom'."

"We found out a few things," Arkady said.

"Have you continued to work with it?"

"Not recently, but this is from reports made to the scientific ethics commission. We've encouraged people to make submissions about current or past projects and it's shaken loose a treasure trove of information. Interestingly, it's come both from Federacy and private projects. I think this is because we've sold ourselves as an independent body, and to an extent, we are. We've been an outlet for scientists who weren't happy with what they're seeing."

"And what have you found out?"

"We've learned that the infection can be present for a long time, but it only gets turned on with light."

"That's true for most multi-cellular organisms," Tina said. "The vast majority of plants only thrive in the presence of light. Most animals depend on light in some form. Do we know whether light makes the host receptive to the infection, makes growth in the host possible, or something else?"

"At this stage, we're not even sure what sort of organism it is."

"It's the ultimate basic form of life," Tina said "It's material from which life is made. I've heard people call it God's putty. All living things could be made from it. Whether it's an animal or plant, it needs nourishment and light provides the energy to turn that nourishment into tissue."

When she was doing experiments with the material, one of the things that worried her was the material's unlimited capability to grow and morph into different types of structures. Given enough light and nourishment, a simple dish with a few specks of dust would produce an incredible amount of tissue in a short period.

She told him about her experiments with Project Charon and how she had first become concerned with the repeated health problems of the people who worked there.

"Do you know that almost no one of the workers there is still alive, apart from you?" he said in a low voice.

"What happened to the others?"

"They died of infections, even after they were promoted out of the Force, and many of them simply disappeared. Of course we know that some of them have gone to the pirates."

"Dexter," Tina said.

"That is the rumour, but I'm not sure I believe it."

"How so? Do you have any evidence?"

"There is no evidence to the contrary. There is no evidence that he went to the pirates."

"But he sold the material to them."

"He sold the material to a company that he might not have

been aware was allied with the pirates, and there are some records that say that he regretted his choice."

"After he was expelled from the Force."

"As it always goes."

Tina wasn't sure how much she believed this. Dexter and remorse didn't go together well. As far as she knew, Dexter had arranged the meeting knowing full well that external companies who wanted to buy the rift dust might not share the Force's ethics and aims. It would have been stupid of him not to think of the consequences.

"When's the last time you saw Dexter?" she asked.

"I'm not entirely sure," Arkady said. "Remember, I was never in the Force and didn't have much contact with any of them, other than that I became interested after my brother met his fate."

"Did you see Dexter after that?"

"I never met him personally, but as a scientist, he was part of some virtual communities where I'm also a member. He burst onto the scene, strutted around exuding a lot of confidence that he was going to solve all the problems in the world, and then he vanished. That was soon after my brother disappeared."

Tina had lost contact with Dexter a few years later, after he paid for Rex's first harness. She'd been angry with him and hadn't kept up the correspondence. Now she felt that maybe she should have. She'd barely read his sparse remarks about what he was doing, back when he might still have hoped the split was temporary.

Arkady continued, "But Dexter is just one of the Project Charon employees that we've failed to locate."

"Jake Monterra," Tina said.

"He's at Kelso Station."

"He's associated with the pirates. He's also still alive."

"That's all I know about him. The pirates are very secretive, and if you're close enough to them that you can see what they're doing, your life is in grave danger. We don't want to give ourselves away, so it all has to be done in secret. It's not that we don't have any information at all, but that we don't know how true some of it is, and it's impossible to check the sources. We can't act on rumours that turn out to be untrue."

"A true scientist," Thor said. He had been silent during most of the discussion. "I think you are all far too careful. I get frustrated with you lot. Meanwhile these people get away with capturing civilians and military personnel and turning them into giant grey octopuses."

Arkady left not much later.

Tina liked to pretend that losing Evelle was nothing to her, that all those arguments in their unit at Project Charon were worth nothing, and that it was perfectly normal for fifteen-year-olds to run away from a safe home. That it wasn't something about her and her terrible skills as a mother. That Evelle was just very independent at a young age and nothing would have kept her home.

But at night, she could still see the moment Evelle walked out the door. She had done it before, and Tina thought nothing of it at the time.

Only much later had she heard that Evelle had taken a shuttle to Pandana where she had signed up while lying about having permission from her parents.

THEY WERE ABOUT to go to bed when Rex announced that he'd received a message from Finn.

"Is anything wrong?" Tina asked.

"He says he managed to crack a private channel and that's why he could send a message. They're still within view of the station. He says Rasa is telling him to unfold the habitat because she's ill all the time. Apparently the geese escaped twice and they've already spent hours trying to vacuum the poop and feathers from the cabin."

"Sounds like a lot of fun."

CHAPTER TWENTY-ONE

AS USUAL, Tina slept poorly because the sounds and smells of the room were unfamiliar to her.

She thought about how Finn and Rasa were getting on with each other and how Finn was dealing with five geese in zero gravity. The ship wouldn't be able to fold out the habitat since they needed to be able to return to the station quickly. Rasa wouldn't like it because she suffered with motion sickness. She had suffered this at the start of the trip, too. At least Tina hoped it was motion sickness and had nothing to do with her activities with Rex in the closed shower cubicle.

After a night of tossing and turning, Tina got up early and snuck out of the room without disturbing Rex.

Thor was already up. "Tea?" he asked.

It was uncanny how he was able to figure out who entered just from listening to her soft footfalls on the ground.

Tina took tea from him. He sat at the table. While drinking tea, they compared notes for bringing up teenage boys. He said Jens was getting to be more independent, and he sometimes feared for what his future might bring. He might accidentally stumble into a difficult situation.

"He just moves so quickly with all the technology," Thor said. "I have trouble getting my hands on stuff so that I can catch up with what he's doing."

Tina hadn't even tried. While Rex was working in his workshop at Gandama, he'd been constantly talking to other people.

"Don't you worry what Jens gets up to occasionally?" Tina asked.

"All the time. He's a good kid. He got a good scare when he discovered that lab and lost his friend, and he knows this is serious business. But I often worry that he's still a kid and will do something dumb."

"What about girls?"

Thor snorted. "He's a bit young for that sort of thing, isn't he?"

"I don't think so."

How easy would it be for Jens to eye the girls. His father couldn't even see what he was doing.

"Does Rex get up to that sort of thing? You know…"

"We have a girl in our crew the same age as him. You know Rasa. I suspect there might be something going on there."

"And you object?"

"I don't object as much as I don't want him to get into trouble."

Thor laughed. "I suspect that without this kind of 'trouble' neither of the two boys would exist."

True. "But Rex is so young. He's just a boy."

"They grow up quickly. Just as well. It's not a kind world. Frankly, the boys could do a lot worse than messing with girls."

Also true. "I just don't want him to suffer for silly mistakes."

"Jens is my mistake. His mother is a bitch. He shouldn't have existed if I'd had half a brain. Yet he's the best thing in my life."

The sound of a door opening came from within the apartment. Jens and Rex came into the living room.

Jens looked from Tina to his father. "Why did you stop talking? Were you talking about us?"

"Of course we were," Thor said. "Because teenage boys are the most important people in the world."

Jens snorted. Rex met Tina's eyes. He was much less a little boy than his friend. Yes, they grew up very quickly.

She should probably let go of her moral panic at the thought of him having sex with a girl. But she was still serious about not letting him blunder into parenthood in the way she had. If she still could.

They had breakfast and then started making plans.

The first trouble was convincing the others that she should go alone. Rex didn't want to hear of it, but she said she'd thought about it a lot and Rex was simply too tall, too visible and too memorable for anyone guarding the entrance to the agricultural section not to notice.

"A middle-aged woman is invisible, especially an ugly, wrinkled middle-aged woman wearing a tool belt. If I say I'm coming to fix something, no one is going to ask questions or suspect I'm up to something. I can easily poke around and pretend I'm lost. That's not so easy when I have this gleaming, strong, threatening companion with me."

"So now I'm too awesome," Rex said.

"You are a lot of things, but ordinary and bland is not one of them."

"But what if someone discovers you and locks you up?"

"It's a last resort, but one way to discover where prisoners are kept is to become one."

Rex, Thor and Jens all protested at the same time.

"You can't do that, Mum," Rex said.

"I can, because I have you. Because you can get into their computer systems. Before I go, I want you two to find out how to disable their systems, and when I give the go ahead, do it."

Rex protested. "So you just want me to sit here behind the computer? You're not exactly making use of my awesomeness here."

"Listen to the second half of the plan."

"It had better be good." But she could hear in his voice that he was enjoying himself.

"All right. I go through the agricultural entrance. But we all know something sinister is going on in some of those chambers. I am going to 'accidentally' blunder into them, and I'll record the experience. You are then going to create a ruckus by sending those recordings to whoever you think will get angry about it."

"That'd be the entire station," Thor said.

"The more people, the better. If you couldn't motivate those scientists to speak out, we'll do it for them. Then they can back up my recordings with their knowledge. Whatever I record, you're going to spread it through the entire station using your awesome knowledge about hacking things. So, basically, we're going to make sure Artan is so busy putting out fires in the station population that he's less likely to notice that his position is compromised in a lot of different ways."

"I don't know about that," Thor said. "That man is extremely dangerous."

"I have no intention of coming face to face with him. He

doesn't know me. I'm just a random maintenance technician and, if I'm asked, I will be a station resident looking for a friend who went missing. I'll be using my second ID."

Rex exclaimed, "No, Mum, you're not going alone! He'll put you into one of those tubes."

"Do I look like I want to turn into a toad? I'm probably worth far more to him alive than dead."

"But only if he knows who you are."

True. Well, there were risks. It was not to be helped. Tina was going to enter the "dark zone" of the station through the docks area by pretending to be an emergency maintenance technician. Thor said he had some friends who might be able to provide her with suitable clothing and other outfits.

She would make sure that the tool kit would contain a few items that could be used as weapon and she would make sure she'd carry some under her clothes as well. One that she particularly liked was a testing rod that you probed into narrow spaces to test the health of connections. It was a long metal rod on a handle. Originally it was intended only to detect currents, but Thor rigged up a powerful battery so that it could stun a person at the slightest touch.

Rex and Jens spent most of the day trying to gain access to as many systems as possible and establishing communication channels.

Tina could, of course, contact Rex through her comms device, but using that would be dumb, because that was the first place people would be looking once she started releasing recordings. So Thor rigged up one of the electronics diagnostic devices to receive messages from his account. He wouldn't let Jens do this, because "I can pretend that I need it for my work, and I don't have a future to protect."

Jens and Rex would operate the account, though.

Tina liked having lots of options, so she insisted on getting other methods of contacting the apartment. Jens scanned her irises, recorded her fingerprints, gave her several passwords and showed her ways to get into the station's systems, including how to send a message to him from several different entry points.

Rex sat next to him, lapping it all up. Tina had a feeling Jens must spend a lot of time waiting around. Since there was no longer a school at Aurora Station, he had nothing to do for most of the day.

She had thought Rex was lonely, but Jens must have been leading a very lonely existence indeed, trailing after his father.

Thor asked for assistance from his circle of friends and the scientific ethics society. Soon, people started arriving at the apartment. Arkady came back, as did Jetta and Yalinda, and with them were a number of other people who introduced themselves as scientists or teachers.

Arkady explained to Tina that these were people in the community who wanted to see action and that they would help spread the information Tina collected.

A woman who was a technician brought her a pair of station maintenance overalls. They carefully detached the tag and Jens printed a tag with her name and a bogus company logo. The woman explained to Tina how people would normally get access to restricted areas and which areas normally saw the most problems.

"It's always recycling," she said. "You can tell the health of a station by looking at the recycling plant."

Based on that, Tina guessed the station's health wasn't great.

It was almost time to go. They had decided to use this time

of day, because it was when activity was winding down and when it was important that technical problems were fixed before people went home and the skeleton crew of the night shift came in.

CHAPTER TWENTY-TWO

BEFORE SHE LEFT, she beckoned Rex to their room. After they both went in, she shut the door and faced him.

He had grown so much and not just by extending his harness. His face had lost the childish look. The stray hairs on his chin would soon need to be cut. Her baby son was a man.

"I know I'm asking a lot of you," she said.

"No, you're keeping me out of a lot of things. You could ask more."

"You, Thor and Jens are my rescue team. If something goes wrong, you'll need to try to get me out. That is a big responsibility. I want you to take that very seriously. It's not nothing I'm asking you to do."

He nodded, his young face serious.

"If something happens, I want you to help Jens and Thor, and listen carefully to what they say. They know the station better than you."

He nodded again.

"If Finn comes back before I return, I want you to tell him where I am. He doesn't need to know the exact details of the plan unless there is a reason for him to know. Show him what you've rigged up with Jens only if he needs to know."

"Don't you trust him?"

"I trust him. I don't trust his family."

His mouth formed into an O.

"There is, however, one thing I want you to do specifically that has nothing to do with Thor or Jens."

Tina went to her bed and gave him the bag that contained all the possessions she had taken from the ship.

"I want you to look after this and, if necessary, use the contents."

The bag was made of soft material. Rex probed it, until his hands met the long shape of the Fireseed still wrapped in her jacket.

His eyes widened. "I thought you said you weren't going to bring it? You said you wouldn't."

"I did. I changed my mind, and Finn didn't want it." And she hadn't wanted to tell anyone else that she had taken the weapon.

"Take it. I hate to ask you this, but you are the strongest of all of us, and the least vulnerable. If it's necessary, protect our friends. Protect Finn and Rasa if they come back. Protect Thor and Jens and take them to the ship."

"I thought it was dangerous to fire weapons inside a closed habitat."

"It is. Keep that in mind."

He nodded again, his face now very serious.

"Please come back safely, Mum." His eyes glittered.

"Of course."

She hugged him, feeling the warmth of his body in between the cold metal of his breastplate and arms. Then she playfully pulled one of the long hairs that sprouted from his chin.

"Ouch."

"Of course I'll come back. Who else will get you your first shaver?"

It was time to go. Tina strapped on her devices, her tool belt, picked up her toolbox and left the apartment. Rex stood at the door and watched her go.

There was so much that Tina wanted to say, that she cared about him, that she wanted him to be happy above all else, that she thought he was growing into a wonderful young man. But he would just raise his eyebrows and wonder why his mother had gone all sentimental.

So she waved to him and hoped she looked confident, because she certainly didn't feel confident.

This was a crazy plan.

Tina walked quickly through the passages to the docks. For all that the station was under lockdown, it was surprisingly busy, with people returning from their jobs as if nothing was going on.

It was amazing how quickly people adapted to new situations and how quickly a stifling situation became the new normal.

By the time she got to the entrance of the docks area, most crowds had dissipated.

A couple of men hung around at the checkpoint, but they didn't appear to be very interested in her. She told them there was a problem with the recycling and that she needed to fix it straight away.

Jens had managed to raise a real technical assistance request, which checked out, and her second ID, with matching company badge, did the trick.

While she waited to go through, a man showed up, wanting to know when a certain passenger ship would arrive. His wife was on it, and he'd been separated from her for more than a year. He got angry when told that no ships were arriving at the docks right now. He showed them the timetable, and started arguing that they couldn't just stop all traffic to the station.

He was very agitated and the discussion, taking place next to Tina, was confronting and personal. A number of extra guards arrived. Tina wondered how long it would be before an altercation broke out.

But her permission came through and she cleared the checkpoint.

Tina was sweating under her jacket. The tool belt felt heavy around her waist.

The dock area looked much tidier, now that it wasn't crowded with hundreds of people waiting for tickets off the station, for jobs in the docks or some other thing. Gone were the crowds, the people hanging around in the passages, the begging and heckling.

This area was all business. Cargo was being delivered, people were having business meetings in a row of offices and meeting rooms. It looked like they'd simply cleared out the common people, leaving only those who had a reason to be in the docks.

Tina took a slight detour through the passages past the SF *Manila*. There was no one at the ship. The door to the entrance tube was closed. The closed-circuit screens displayed a couple of empty corridors and the deserted bridge. The ship data screen said eighty-five percent readiness.

It was really strange, because when a ship prepared for departure, all kinds of tasks needed to be performed by the crew. There would be junior pilots on the bridge putting the ship through tests. There would be people walking around checking all the ship's power modules. As far as she could see, no one was performing those tasks. It was very strange. Just what did the pirates plan to do with the ship, because they obviously wanted to use it soon?

Someone entered the passage behind her, so Tina kept going in the direction of the agricultural sector.

The passage to this part of the station went through a fairly narrow corridor with a security door at the end. The guards letting her into the docks had given her a temporary access card, and it opened the door as they said it would.

It was odd how some of the station's operations were in a state of chaos, but others were well-organised. It worried Tina that she had no idea if the well-organised parts were the original station systems, or if they were pirate-installed systems.

She would really like to think that the pirates were poorly organised, but a number of facts pointed to at least some of the pirate systems being better than the original station's operations.

The security door led into the agricultural sector. The air was humid here, and laced with the familiar earthy scent that accompanied living plants. The main growing areas comprised several levels of racks containing a meshlike tube network that held the crops. Banks of lights hung on the bottom of each shelf to illuminate the plants that grew underneath. Here and there, clouds of humidity issued from sprinklers that came on and switched off by themselves.

Tina walked along the central aisle, looking up at all the greenery surrounding her. The plants were mostly fruit and salad vegetables, which meant there was likely a bigger room somewhere else.

The farms were usually restricted areas in most stations, but most stations also had greenhouses. Yet she remembered very clearly coming to Peris City for the first time, and being amazed at the size and abundance of plants—even if Peris City was a rather dry place. She remembered thinking that her life had been so much poorer without plants, and this was why she'd started growing cactuses. Because more than anything, plants made her feel alive.

The nursery was at the very end of the farm hall. She walked past labs filled with tubes with little plants that would later be planted in larger installations. It was all very familiar. Every station where she had lived had this kind of setup. They even had it in her hometown in Tirkala because the desert didn't provide enough food. They kept animals, which were a local species, but the vegetation in the dry landscape was not very nutritious.

The bright lights and green haze over the labs was very familiar to Tina. This was the environment in which she had lived and worked for so long.

At the end of the nursery, she came to the main farm. The size of it took her breath away. The space was so big that it was easy to see the curvature of the station's floor. Layers and layers of growing shelves radiated soft green light. Little robots moved in between the crops, watering them and spraying them with nutrients, and harvesting. A little cart trundled past, full of bright red tomatoes.

A number of people worked on the growing shelves and in the processing plant.

Aurora Station was massive, and this farm was a huge operation, bigger than Tina had ever seen. She made a few recordings, although this was not an area of immediate interest.

The workers she passed did not pay her any attention. In her station overalls, carrying a toolbox, they didn't need to ask what she was doing. She didn't see a single pirate.

She stopped to look at her map, because the recycling plant was somewhere around here. It showed that this area went on into a number of chambers, and that she would have to traverse all of them in order to get to the area that would allow her access to the area beyond the dark zone of the agricultural plant.

At the end of the massive growing chamber another short passage led to a multistorey room with large vats, filters and aeration tanks of the recycling plant. So at the end of that chamber, she went into the next one.

And she stopped at the door.

It was dark in the room beyond and her eyes struggled to make out just what she was seeing.

CHAPTER TWENTY-THREE

THIS ROOM WAS VERY different from the previous. The first thing that Tina noticed, having come from the bright and green farm, was how humid and dark it was inside here.

Pale-blue light emanated only from rows of lights on the gallery levels. There were no bright overhead lights as in the agriculture section.

The room looked a lot more crowded, and this was because gallery levels seemed closer together and were crowded. They contained big chunky boxes with curved glass lids. Row upon row of these things occupied the gallery levels as far as she could see.

In the agriculture sector, the air had been filled with the hisses of water from sprinklers, the zoom of harvesting robots, the clatter of little carriages on the rails. In this room, Tina could hear herself breathe.

She barely dared move, because her footsteps sounded so loud.

She checked her map. According to the data, she was still in the "dark zone".

As she peered at the screen, a message from Rex flashed across.

Are you all right?

She resisted replying immediately. Instead, she kept recording everything she saw. She'd send it to Rex and Jens soon.

She had to wait until her eyes became accustomed to the low light. Standing in the aisle that traversed the sector, she recorded the sheer size of the room, the many gallery levels, the banks of equipment on the ground floor.

Then she slowly climbed up a set of metal stairs that led to the first gallery level, where two rows of the big, chunky cabinets occupied most of the space, leaving just a narrow aisle between them.

Tina peeked through the glass of the first cabinet and almost gasped aloud.

A man was inside. He lay on his back, his eyes closed. Most of his body was covered by a blanket. A few clear tubes came out from under the blanket and disappeared into the side of the cabinet. The area above his head glowed with soft purple light. The fuzz of beard on his chin indicated that he had been in here for a few days, but otherwise he looked like a perfectly healthy young man. He couldn't have been in here for long.

In the next cubicle lay another man in a similar condition, and the same with the next one and the one after that.

She walked along the row, recording everything she saw.

In the fourth cabinet, someone had left open a small panel cover on the outside. Inside was a screen that indicated the temperature inside the chamber, a number of dates and a name: Joshan.

Tina figured out how to open this panel on the next cabinet. This man's name was Lokthar and the next one was Markan. All names that sounded ominously like Artan.

They were all men, and all within the age range that served in active duty in the Force. What was the bet that these were crew from the SF *Manila*?

In her time in the Force, some of the men would tattoo their recruitment numbers on their bodies, usually on their arms, but some would have the number on the side of their necks, under the ear.

And indeed, a few cabinets later, she found a young man with a number on the side of his neck. She took a photo of him showing his face, making sure the number in the picture was legible.

At the end of the section of the gallery, where a narrow metal bridge connected it to the next gallery, was a desk with a computer screen. Tina crouched under the desk, disconnected the cables and connected them to the electrical diagnostics tool as Jens had shown her. She used her fingerprint to authenticate access, and sent the recordings she had made.

A moment later, Jens sent back the recruitment card of the man in question:

Brett Finlayson, age twenty-six, place of origin: Olympus, time in the Force: three years and two months. Employment: SF *Manila*.

Her heart jumped.

Tina went back to look at the young man's face and spotted what she hadn't seen the first time: a faded bruise on his forehead. This young man had not asked to be put in this tube.

She walked along the rows of the next gallery. Most of the occupants here, too, had been inside for only a few days at most. They were all men. Where were the female crew of the ship?

She had to find them.

As Tina walked, the level of technology and content of the cabinets started to change.

The first men she saw were just asleep, but later ones were attached to machinery that monitored things she didn't understand. Clear fluid was being pumped into their veins.

A while later, she noticed how the men who had been in for more than three months started to change. Their skin became grey and mottled, and then warty.

Some men were left in this state, with all equipment removed except whatever kept them in stasis, and others continued to receive treatment. Some of them grew into grotesque shapes, with their hands changing into multi-tentacled octopuses, and their faces becoming unrecognisable as human. Their skin started to darken from light grey to slate grey.

Tina stopped and recorded the vastness of the hall.

There were at least fifty of these cabinets on this section of the gallery. Each gallery consisted of at least ten of these sections, maybe more, but it got too dark at the far end of the huge chamber for her to see. There were at least six gallery levels on this side of the chamber, and another six on the other. That meant there were about six thousand men being turned into warty toads.

Then she came to a group of people who were barely recognisable as human. Their clothes had been cut away from them, showing that the protuberances grew all over their skin. One of these people had been frozen, with a layer of rime lining the tentacles. Tina wondered why that was. Had the person not survived the experiment? Or were they able to freeze people and revive them later? Or was that the experiment they were doing here?

Arkady had said that the people with the more grotesque modifications were the strongest.

She remembered seeing the monkey-like creature in her backyard, sick at the thought that this might once have been a human.

And these people had made the effort to come to her at Gandama to get their hands on the cactuses or on her and Rex for their experiments. Maybe once these creatures were released from these cubicles, they were slaves to their masters.

She felt sick.

It was really quiet in this room, with only the occasional hiss of air going into the capsules, a very low hum of the equipment, and the usual distant clicks and clangs as the station rotated and moved into and out of sunlight.

She collected images and sent them to Jens, hoping that Thor's friends and their families would be angry enough to demand answers.

The pirates were doing this to innocent people. Perhaps they had done it to the people who had gone missing at the station.

But there were so many of them. What other stations did the pirates have? How many of these people would they need to populate their army? Could she afford to wait doing something about this until she managed to get to Olympus?

Her gut feeling said probably not.

How long would it take before the change in these men's bodies was irreversible? How long would they have to lie here in these cabinets under these blue lights—hang on. Hadn't she observed some strange changes in her cactuses when grown under artificial light aboard the *Alethia*? Grow lights in a ship habitat often had a higher concentration of UV than sunlight, because it strengthened the structure of the stems so they didn't go too floppy in lower gravity. That was it: the third DNA strand mutation was activated by exposure to ultraviolet light. Arkady had said that his work pointed in that direction.

So what if... she just turned all these lights off? And then turned off the other machines so that the men weren't kept asleep?

But where to do that?

Jens would be able to find out.

Tina found another workstation, connected her diagnostic screen and wrote a message explaining what she wanted. Turn off the power to this room. Try to do it in a way that was not immediately obvious. He might be able to just turn off the galleries at the end of the room where she had entered, disabling just the cabinets that contained the *Manila* crew.

But before she was able to send it, there was a soft sound behind her.

She whirled around.

Two men stood behind her. She had no weapon, because anything that could be used as such was in her tool kit and there was no time to unpack it. It was too late to run.

"What are you doing here?"

The man looked unfamiliar. He was wearing a uniform, but unlike any Tina had ever seen. The material was made from a metallic type of fabric that sat snugly over his body. He looked very shapely, with wide shoulders and muscled arms.

His partner had grey mottled skin, but still looked human.

"I have an order to make some repairs. I think I got lost and I was just asking my boss where I need to go."

Tina glanced at her comm device. Whatever happened, she needed to send that message to Jens.

"Where is your authorisation?"

"Hang on, I'll show it to you."

Tina pressed "send" on the message to Jens. She hoped she'd filled in all the relevant details, like his address. Then she wiped the screen and pulled up the fake maintenance order Jens had made for her. She showed it to the men.

They frowned.

"That's in the recycling plant next door. You're in the wrong place."

"Oh. Sorry. I'm new."

He gave her a suspicious look. "How did you get in anyway?"

"The door was open, and there was no one to ask if I was in the right place," Tina said.

"This is a restricted area."

"I understand, but as I said, the door was open."

"Hmm. Did you get a pass to get into the ag sector?"

"I did."

He held out his hand, and Tina handed it to him, much as she didn't want to give it. He inserted the pass into a reader and showed the screen to his colleague, who nodded, but said nothing.

Tina's heart was hammering.

"We'll be keeping this."

"But I need to get into the right place."

"You don't need the pass to get *out* of a restricted area."

"I need to fix—"

"Go back to the checkpoint and apply for a new pass."

"I'll have to go and talk to my boss."

"You do that."

Tina shouldered her toolkit bag and walked past the two men. Her legs trembled when she went down the stairs to the ground floor.

What should she do?

If she went back to the apartment, they would follow her and find out about Thor and Jens. If she went back to the checkpoint, they would refuse a second permit, and they would look into who issued the first one.

She didn't need the pass to get *out* of the restricted area. But now she was already in the restricted area...

The two men were still on the gallery level. They couldn't see her from where they were.

Tina checked her comm device. The message to Jens had disappeared off the screen, but he had not yet replied. Had he received it?

Heavy footsteps on the metal floor of the gallery above indicated that the two men were coming towards the stairs.

Tina made a snap decision.

Instead of heading back to the recycling plant, she turned the other way and walked deeper into the restricted area, keeping to the side and making sure she was out of sight of the bottom of the stairs.

It wasn't long before a male voice called out. "Hey! Where did she go?"

Tina ran.

CHAPTER TWENTY-FOUR

A MALE VOICE shouted behind her.

Tina made sure that she kept out of the line of vision, ducking behind banks of equipment and pallets with supplies. She would have loved to have had more time to look around. What was in the large bottles packed neatly in a metal cage? What did the machine with the blinking lights do? A number of white tubes ran from it into the ceiling, presumably to the people in the cabinets on the shelf above.

But there was no time to look.

The men had figured out that she had run in the wrong direction, further into the restricted area. They were somewhere behind her, but she couldn't see how far.

Tina reached the far end of the hall.

The main passage was blocked by a solid door that was closed, but a small door next to it was open.

She ran in, plunging into utter darkness. With her hands along the wall, she managed to proceed a couple of steps, but then her hands met a corner, and she couldn't work out if it was a right angle or there was a cupboard in the passage.

She pressed herself against the wall, her heart thudding. She fumbled for her tool belt. At such close range, she would have to use the stunner. She hoped it had lost little of its charge.

The entrance into the large hall showed up like a grey rectangle, dotted with a few glows of purple light.

A silhouette stopped at the door. Tina grabbed the handle of the makeshift stunner, waving the business end in front of her.

If the man came into the passage alone, she might have a chance, but if they both came, not even a miracle was going to save her.

The man said something to his comrade. It sounded like some dialect of Sinolese and Tina wasn't good at Sinolese, especially the informal type.

She grabbed the handle with sweaty hands.

Come, come a bit closer.

She pushed herself along the wall towards the entrance. She did not want to get stuck here. This passage might lead somewhere, but she couldn't see it, and she couldn't make a light because they would know where she was.

Come on, come a bit closer... a bit closer...

Tina hit out with the stunner. The zap of electricity was so loud that she could feel it through the handle. The man didn't even have time to yell out. He dropped to the ground with a heavy thud.

Tina didn't wait for his colleague to come over to check. She ran out of the passage—straight into the second person.

Something soft and sticky lashed around her arms. Tentacles. Eew. Eeeeeew.

She hit out with the rod, hitting soft and springy threads. They lost grip on her arm.

Tina ran.

She ran past the large closed door. She didn't know where she was going or what had happened to the second person.

There was another entrance on the other side of the large closed roller door. A ceiling light cast a pale glow within the depth of the passage. It was impossible to tell where it went. Some sort of maintenance corridor, she guessed. Maybe the inner shelter of the station that Jens had been talking about.

She ran.

The passage looked deserted. There were no doors to either side, just a metal walkway suspended over a set of pipes. She chanced a glance over her shoulder. A person was just coming into the entrance.

She spotted a recess in the space under the walkway. She climbed over the railing, stepped onto the pipe and jumped down.

Only when she had ducked into the dark niche that held a control panel did she realise that she might have a hard time climbing back up.

But she'd worry about that later.

Footsteps thudded on the metal walkway, becoming louder. They weren't very fast footsteps, and as they came closer, the sound of muffled voices became clear. The footsteps were kind of uneven and limping.

Tina pressed herself as far into the alcove as possible. She sat well within the shadows.

The two men came past, one supporting the other. They spoke softly and stopped regularly to look around. But they passed Tina without spotting her.

Tina waited as quietly as she could until they were out of sight.

As she had suspected, getting back up on the walkway

proved a bit of a challenge. She had to track back quite a bit before she found a spot where there was a joint in the pipes with a rim and bolts that she could use to haul herself up.

During this time, no one came into the passage.

The light remained on, which probably meant a motion sensor kept it on for her, and this might also mean that someone was watching into the passage through a remote channel. She needed to find something quickly, because any warnings that her presence generated would escalate the longer she stayed here.

At the end of the passage she came to a T-intersection. Her map told her that if she turned left, she might end up in a wider passage that was part of the main thoroughfare, presuming the door between the two was open.

Tina found the door and tried it, but it was locked. So she kept going. How long would it be before she ran into those two men who had passed her? They weren't going very fast. They might have warned their mates.

No, she needed a better disappearing trick.

When she passed a narrow ladder going up, she took that option, and on the landing at the top of the stairs, she checked her map again.

From what she could gather, she was now on top of the main thoroughfare that she hadn't been able to get into. The tubes that ran along here were likely to be filtered air coming from the recycling plant back in the "dark zone" and there should now be signs of people in the passage underneath her. She walked along, looking for a vent where sound would come up. When she found one, the air going through the duct made so much noise that any noise from the passage was drowned out. Well, that wasn't much use.

She considered going back down the ladder, but that was just going to put her into the path of people looking for her.

The map told her that the passage underneath her led past several local authority establishments, like education and health care offices and after that past a primary school.

A station this size would have several schools, nothing like the small school at Project Charon that Evelle had attended, where most education was done remotely anyway.

The next sector was a medical precinct. The walkway zigzagged in between structures poking up from below, likely related to imaging equipment. She also came past a vent where she definitely heard voices. They were men, and it sounded like they were in some sort of heated discussion. No matter how much she listened, she couldn't make out any words.

The next vent was closer to the source, and the discussion was clearer, but it was conducted in a language Tina didn't understand, something like Transigian or Vertolian.

One man was not happy, though. Apart from his raised voice, there was also some banging, as if they were kicking a door or wall.

Someone else shouted, "Shut up!" which was followed by a heavy clang, like the shutting of a door.

What was the chance that this was where people were kept prisoner? Was there a way she could get in?

Tina looked around, but all she could find was a control panel.

Using Jens' diagnostic tool, she managed to break into the local computer system. It showed the existence of several video inputs, likely to be security cameras, because she recognised the model numbers. Infrared cameras.

They showed her live images of dorm rooms, each occupied by a number of people. From the way they sat and walked Tina guessed they were all men. Not the crew from the *Manila*, but possibly captives from earlier missions.

Jens confirmed that the area had been a school and that the men were locked up in the classrooms. She asked if Jens could make the door locks malfunction.

He told her that since her last contact with him, he had managed to dig up an override routine that he could send if she thought she could use it.

Tina said she could. She didn't know how good it was going to be. Most security systems were robust enough to have at least some resistance to these types of hacks but maybe bringing down the entire system was not what she wanted anyway.

So he sent the routine, and Tina recorded the specifics of the cameras and the locking mechanisms. They definitely seemed a little primitive. She presumed that a detailed security system had not been part of the original school.

She was working on a plan. Maybe she didn't even need to go into the main part of the station. If this passage continued and led past all the now-closed institutions where the pirates kept prisoners, then maybe she could find out how their security systems worked and disable all of them at once.

If all the prisoners got out at the same time, the place would descend into utter chaos, and Tina could escape with Evelle, if she could find her, and the others still capable of escaping.

She would need help.

The big question was whether any Federacy ships were nearby that could pounce the moment riots broke out, and help them, or if there would be enough pirates at the station to deal with prisoners running riot in the station. She would like to answer the last question in the negative, but these strange modified people were said to be super-strong.

Any Federacy ships in the area wouldn't advertise their presence so she was unlikely to find out if there were any until chaos in the station happened.

It was a gamble.

Tina sat down on the walkway and looked at Jens' routine. It was indeed very simple and she didn't think it would work, but then she remembered that she had a library of code snippets that she had written herself to overcome problems in clients' systems.

If she took Jens' code to break in and then appended some of her code and inserted the security passcodes she had just pilfered from the ex-school's system, maybe the computers could be fooled into thinking that the break-in code was just a regular verification request.

Yes, that might work.

Tina tried it on the school system below her, and she got in all the way to the central command module. No, it clearly wasn't a school anymore. She found lists of how many people were kept in which rooms.

Jens gave her an updated map which included observations she had passed to him. Ironically, she hadn't ventured far from the agriculture plant, and this looked like a viable escape route, but if a whole bunch of people tromped through there, alarms would definitely start ringing. So they only got one chance going out that way, and there needed to be as many people as possible.

Tina kept going.

She found a couple of other places that had been turned into hostels or prisons: the high school, the administrative offices and the hospital. The latter was a multi-storey affair with a central atrium. The map showed it consisted of hundreds of rooms and Jens said that the concentration of people in that area appeared to be quite high.

She managed to plant the routine and penetrate deep into the security system, but once again didn't find any names. The people appeared to be identified by number. She needed a way to translate numbers into names.

On the other side of the hospital was the old data centre and the place Jens had identified as the likely headquarters for Artan and his cronies. Sadly, the maintenance passage didn't go directly over that area, but passed instead over a commercial area.

What a pity. How awesome would it be if she could break into the central command module?

She studied the map again to see if she could get access to that room in some other way. It was an area of the station where a spoke attached to the ring structures that formed the habitat.

The spokes contained goods lifts in and out of zero-g storage, structures necessary for the integrity of the station and often industrial plants that didn't require a large workforce—or even any workforce—to operate.

Tina walked around the area where the spoke structure met the ring and she found an access panel that led to a narrow emergency passage to the level below. While she was climbing, a lift rumbled past on the other side of the spoke wall, close enough to make her jump.

The emergency access tube came out in a small, cramped space with another access panel. She carefully pushed it out so that she could see through the crack between the panel and the wall. It was quite dark in the room beyond, and she had to press her nose against the panel in order to see through the narrow strip.

In the semidarkness stood banks of computers with workstations, unoccupied. Evidence for the fact that the pirates attempted to run the station with too few people?

She pushed the door further open, holding the stunner with one hand. But there was no one in the dark room. She spotted two security cameras, but if she made straight for the bank of control stations, she could duck between the benches.

Tina took the wall panel out and set it next to the entrance, in case she needed to get back out in a hurry. Then she ventured into the room. She ducked between the workstations to stay out of view of the cameras.

Using the screen from the diagnostics tool, she uploaded lists of numbers to try to match them with names.

The database spat out a long list of data that, on the little screen, scrolled by too quickly for her to read. But it looked like it might be useful. Great.

Now she just needed to—

Someone grabbed her from behind.

CHAPTER TWENTY-FIVE

TINA MANAGED TO STIFLE A SQUEAK. Her right arm was pinned since the attacker had grabbed her by the wrist. But Tina knew a trick for that. With her free hand, she grabbed the attacker by the wrist and twisted her arm. He had to let go.

She yanked the stunner from her belt and lashed out at him. The metal rod connected, sending a shower of sparks into the air. He yelled and fell backwards, clutching his arm.

The man was taller than her and had mottled skin.

Tina had to stop him coming after her or warning others. She grabbed the back of the nearest chair intending to knock him unconscious with it—only to find it was bolted onto the ground.

She ran back to the emergency access and grabbed the cover of the panel. By now, an alarm was ringing. Also, the man had recovered from her strike with the stunner, and he now had help from two mates.

Tina had nowhere to run. She tried to back into the emergency access, but two men came from the sides and cut off her exit. She tried to keep them at bay by swinging the panel cover, but one of them simply yanked it out of her hands. She stunned one with the rod, but the other two had her pinned against the wall pretty soon.

With their weight pressing against her, she couldn't move. Their bodies were warm and heavy, the infected and mottled skin far too close for her liking. They said she was supposed to be immune, but who knew?

The men spoke a heavy Sinolese dialect, and Tina's questions went ignored.

They dragged her in between the banks of workstations, all of them empty. If this was a control centre, they weren't controlling much here.

They reached the far end of the room and went out the security door.

The passage on the other side looked normal. The lights worked, the floor was clean and people went about their business normally.

There were not quite as many people as in the unrestricted part of the station. Many of the people had mottled skin. None of them looked twice at three burly guys frogmarching a middle-aged woman between them.

Where were they taking her?

In the scuffle in the control room, she had lost her tool bag and was left only with what she carried on her belt. At some point, they would remove that, too, and then she'd lose her easiest way of communicating with Rex, Jens and Thor. They didn't even know what was going on yet and she couldn't warn them until these thugs let her go. And if they took her belt, she would have to find another device to communicate. From some kind of prison, that wouldn't be easy.

The men took her along passageways with rooms to the side. Whenever doors were open, Tina could see people in those rooms at work or in meetings. Most of them were of the warted and grey skin type.

They came to a large open area, dimly lit, with a floor of smooth, rubbery material. A couple of seats were in the middle, surrounded by a bank of screens.

One of the seats was occupied by a man with grey warty skin. Another seat was also occupied, but Tina could only see a pair of legs, since the chair faced away from her.

The screens displayed feeds from security cameras in the station, including the agricultural sector, the docks, the residential areas, the commercial passages, the large hall where the Ship Supply office was, and even the area immediately outside the station.

Here she was thinking that anything that happened on the station was a secret. She would have been picked up the moment the *Alethia* entered the station's influence.

At their approach, the chair facing away swivelled around.

And in it sat a man who Tina recognised immediately. His skin was dark rusty-red and, rather than warty, it was smooth and looked wet, like a frog's skin.

Hundreds of tentacles hung from the line of his jaw, constantly getting longer or shorter and slowly swaying from side to side. The top of his head was bald, save for a couple of thicker tentacles that branched into thinner ones. Those moved all the time, too. The jacket he wore over a loose singlet showed that his chest was equally smooth and red-skinned. An amulet crafted from what looked like hair dangled from his pirate belt, as well as a knife.

His hands, if you could still call them that, rested on the armrests of the chair. Tentacles also covered the backs of his hands, making them look like unruly mops. He wore loose trousers. His feet were bare, with long curved nails like those of a dog.

She imagined that in times past, when people had imagined the devil, he would have looked surprisingly like the creature she saw before her.

This was the pirate leader Artan.

He laughed. "You already know me. Why don't you bow?"

"I don't bow for criminals."

One of the tentacles on his hands shot out. By the time it wrapped around Tina's arm, it had stretched to a thin cord, but the strength in it made her gasp. It pulled at her, but she resisted.

The men who had brought her forced her to kneel onto the ground. Tina fell unceremoniously. A pain shot through her knee even though the floor was quite bouncy. Sitting on her knees had never been a strong point of hers.

Artan casually flicked his fingers. The tentacle that surrounded her flicked loose and flew back to him. It became part of his hand.

"So you thought you were smart," he said.

It was impossible to see his mouth where the sound was coming from. Just about everything on his face moved constantly, and she had the impression that those tentacles were sizing her up. Those ones on the top of his head ended in little bulbs with a black spot inside, like snail eyes.

"Bow further," one of the guards said.

When Tina refused, he whacked her head from behind.

The contact with his fleshy tentacles made her shudder.

Artan said, "Leave her. She is worth more to me undamaged than damaged. Take her possessions and wait at a distance."

One man took off Tina's belt. When the weight fell off her

hips, panic overcame her. She'd known this was going to happen. It would make contacting Thor so much harder.

Tina rose to her feet. "Excuse me, but I have bad knees. Kneeling doesn't agree with me."

He laughed. "Always defiant." In amongst all the tentacles, she wasn't even sure where his mouth was.

There was something eerily familiar about him, but she was sure she had never met the man Jackson Hirsh, delegate to the Federacy Assembly.

"Tina Freeman. I didn't think I ever had the honour of meeting you."

How did he know who she was?

He laughed. "You thought I wouldn't notice your visit? You know those alias identities of the Federacy Force officers are stored in the Assembly database. That database is small enough to fit inside this tentacle."

He lifted one of the tentacles from his hands. It looked like a worm.

"I know about all those names: Louise Metvier, David Metz, huh? Very interesting person. Rasa Vichenko? Seriously, where do you collect those people?"

Tina's heart was hammering. She would have expected him to know Finn's family, but Rasa?

"Then of course you meet up with the Olafsens. They've been on our watch list for a long time. A lot of rabble you've collected around you, even Arkady Dimitrov!" He laughed. "All the bleeding hearts and do-gooders."

"What is it you actually want?"

He laughed again. "In this room, I ask the questions."

Well then, why wasn't he asking them?

"I am amused, though, why you bleeding hearts can't seem to grasp the concept of progress."

"By progress, you mean occupying innocent people's homes and turning them into warty toads?"

"Tina, Tina." He shook his head. "I thought you, of all people, would understand the potential of this mutation. We can turn ourselves into anything we want, defy any disease and heal any injury."

And why then had he chosen to look like a disgusting slimy toad? She said, "I know about the potential but also know the danger. Not everyone survives contact with the rift material."

"No, sadly, they don't, especially women. We need women, right? Wrong!" He laughed again. It was becoming pretty annoying.

"I have no idea what you're getting at." The infection was said to mess with people's minds. No wonder he didn't make any sense.

From the corner of her eye, she spotted that one of the two men wanted to come closer, probably for punishing her for her transgression or rudeness to their leader. But he waved them away.

"Do relax. This woman amuses me."

Well, Tina found it anything but amusing.

He leaned back in his seat. "Let's get down to business."

"I have no business here. Lock me up if you want to." In fact, the sooner he did that, the sooner she could try to contact Thor.

"You might listen to me before you dismiss me. Unless you know of the Federacy's plans for Project Charon?"

Plans?

"Ha, you don't know. Then listen and be amazed."

He let a silence lapse as if for effect. He was certainly a capable actor. And Tina was determined not to fall into the trap of looking interested. This was a carefully rehearsed act by a cunning man and she should not let his strange appearance distract her or trick her into feeling sorry for him.

"I was a member of the Federacy Assembly many years ago. I was not influential or important, and the world I represented was small and insignificant, an agricultural outpost much like Tirkala."

He had certainly done his research about her, even if all this would have been public knowledge. He wanted to unsettle her.

"I went to Olympus full of ideals, but as happens commonly, the reality didn't live up to them. The Assembly delegates are corrupt, selfish and don't care about the good of the worlds they represent. They go to Olympus to enrich themselves and then to nick off when their time is up, rather than to return home to pass on their knowledge to the people there. I suspect the Force is full of these types of people."

Yes. Dexter was one.

"The interdimensional rift was discovered before you or I were born. The date of the discovery varies according to who you're talking to; it's one of the Federacy's great secrets. In those early days, experiments were pretty extravagant. People used to fly into the rift and come back."

"That's nonsense." That was what conspiracy theorists liked to believe.

"Who told you that?"

"Everyone in the Force knows it. Those ridiculous stories have been around for years, but they're not true and no one can prove it."

"How do you know for sure?" He pulled out a reader and showed her a photo of a battered-up ship, an ancient model that hadn't been around for ages.

"What does that prove?" Tina had not seen the photo before, but had seen ones like it.

He then showed her an image of a man lying on a table—was he dead?—with growths all over his body. Just looking at the image made Tina's skin crawl.

"That's horrific but proves nothing. These could be from anything. I've studied this rift and I've never seen these pictures." Heck they could even have been doctored pictures.

"That's because the Force doesn't want you to see them."

"That's ridiculous. They paid me to study the material. We took a lot more care with our people than this." She gestured at the screen. "We didn't let anyone get into contact with it."

"They paid you to put a respectable face on a sordid piece of history. They paid you so they could pretend they were doing good research to keep humanity safe from this infection."

"What do you even base this nonsense on?" He was nothing but a conspiracy theorist.

He flicked to another picture, this one showing a row of bodies in the dirt, all of them with mottled skin. There were at least a hundred, men, women and children, laid out in rows. In the background was a fence and a line of trees. Another picture involving the supposed infection that she had never seen before. "Have you ever been to Earth?"

"I haven't." She assumed the picture was taken there.

"You would find it interesting. The Federacy tried to kill off a huge part of the population by letting the infection loose, then tried to cover up their actions when it became clear they had done this and people were outraged."

"That's ridiculous. The Federacy is funding projects to find a cure."

"Because they can make money from pretending there is a cure. By feeding into people's fear."

An unsettling feeling crept over her. Finn had said some of those things.

"And then why are you infecting people on purpose?"

"Because there is no cure. The infection is simply another step in the evolution of the human species. We need to embrace it. We will be a varied, powerful species with useful abilities. You look at me and I can see the revulsion in your eyes. But consider this."

He reached for his belt and pulled out a gun. As his tentacles extended further and further towards her, Tina made out that it was a Fireseed, the same model as the battered old weapon she had given to Rex.

He held the weapon so close she could touch it.

"Take it," he said, and laughed. "Take it and shoot me."

Tina resisted the urge. He wouldn't offer it so provocatively to her if there wasn't a catch. The Fireseeds were simple weapons, and they weren't nearly as powerful as the plasma weapons like the Q-blaster. They could kill an ordinary person in most circumstances, but if hit at an awkward angle, or the person wore armour, the result could well be different. Heck, maybe these mutants had grown armour inside their bodies.

She looked at the weapon, but didn't touch it, because that was what he wanted. She wasn't going to do what he wanted.

"Hmph." He gave a small snort and with a flick of his tentacles, withdrew the weapon back to his belt. "You've seen a demonstration before?"

"Yes." She had no idea what he was talking about, presumably a mutant surviving being shot.

"Then you know of the advantages of the new human condition. That's good. Because then I don't have to explain why I would be happy if you could work with us. You have a lot of knowledge that we could use."

Tina stifled a snort of laughter. Well, that was something entirely different than what she had expected to hear. She'd have expected to be put inside one of those cabinets, not to work on the people inside. "The people you're transforming did not ask for it."

"They'll appreciate it."

"They're prisoners. No matter what good you say you do, you can't change that. Those people have not agreed to whatever treatment you give them. I'll have no part in that."

"I would urge you to consider this."

"You cannot pay me enough to do that." She gave him a hard stare. "I'd die before I helped someone who turned people into toads against their will."

"Pity. You would be paid well. I know you can use the money. Well, then, we have plenty of ways to make you change your mind. Be warned: the deal gets worse each time we mention it."

He gave a sign, and the three men approached. Two of them each grabbed hold of one of her arms and led her out of the room.

CHAPTER TWENTY-SIX

ONE WAY TO discover the prison's location was to be taken there yourself. It wasn't the way Tina had preferred, but she no longer had a choice in the matter.

The men marched her out of the room. She was taken down in the lift and along a dark corridor, where the rooms on either side appeared to be unoccupied or contained items for storage.

She imagined the map of the station in her mind while they walked. This area was the administrative area, possibly part of the high school.

Indeed, one room contained rows of seats and screens, as if it was a classroom. They also went past a courtyard with benches surrounding a planter box. She could imagine students sitting there on a break. The tree in the box was dead, the leaves brown and drooping from the branches.

Tina smelled the prison before she got there. A dank scent of human waste and sweat met them while they walked towards what she guessed to be the old hospital.

They entered the central atrium, a hall four floors high,

with galleries on each level. As soon as the door thudded shut behind them, people started yelling. Most voices were muffled by walls and doors and it was impossible to hear what they said, but some prisoners shouted obscenities. All the voices were male, many of them foreign.

A couple of pirates milled around on the ground floor, ignoring the shouts from the prisoners. They spoke briefly in Sinolese with the men who brought Tina, so she didn't understand what they said. They were rough types with mottled skin. One of them carried a security reader on his belt. Tina recognised the model, because she used to sell them in her shop. It wasn't a terribly advanced model, in line with the other security equipment she had seen.

The men then took Tina up one level into a dark gallery, where the guard used the security reader to open a metal door. Pretty old-fashioned.

The men pushed Tina into the darkness of the room.

One of them said something and laughed.

Tina stumbled a few steps. The stench of sweat in the room was so strong that it almost made her gag. It brought back memories of sitting sardined in a transport ship where the air circulation was less than ideal, with people who were on their first trip and were nervous, motion sick, or both.

Smells were always so much stronger inside closed environments.

Tina sensed the presence of other people in the room before the men slammed the door shut behind her.

It was so dark that purple spots danced before her eyes.

After a while a little light went on. Tina squinted in that direction.

A woman said, "Don't waste any power."

"It's a newcomer," another woman said.

Their voices sounded educated.

Another light flicked on.

The same woman as before said, "What did I tell you about not wasting power?"

"We're all going to be dead in a few days anyway," another woman said.

Several female voices told her to stop saying things like that.

A woman closer to Tina said, "Where did you come from?"

"They caught me wandering in the station in a place I shouldn't be."

"You're not Force?"

"I used to be, a long time ago."

"Did you come in with any of the Federacy ships?"

A woman elsewhere in the darkness said, "We don't even know that the Federacy has sent anyone to get us out."

Tina asked, "Are you crew from the Star Fighter *Manila*?"

A brief silence.

Then a woman asked, "Do you know the ship?"

"I served in the Force. I saw it was brought in. I saw you being led away as prisoners." Her heart was hammering. "Is there anyone here called Evelle Freeman?"

Another silence.

"Who wants to know?" a different voice said.

This was a younger woman. Her voice sounded strangely familiar to Tina. But they were still shining the light in her eyes and she couldn't see the faces of all those in this cell.

"Evelle?"

One of the women came closer. Tina could see the uniform and boots and trousers of the wearer, but nothing above the waist.

After another silence in which Tina could imagine her studying Tina's face, the young woman said, "Mum?"

"Evelle."

The young woman touched Tina's shoulder, and Tina pulled her into a hug. It felt as awkward as hell. This was not at all the way Tina had envisaged meeting up with her daughter.

She was so tall and so skinny. She smelled of dirty uniforms and sweat, as did everyone in this room.

"Mum, what are you doing here?"

"Aren't you just a little bit glad to see me?"

"Well no, because we're all going to die in here."

"No we're not," Tina said. "Not if I can help it." But she sounded a lot more confident than she felt. First she would have to find a way to get in contact with Rex and Thor.

Not only that, if she managed to get Evelle out, she would also have to free all these other women and the bigger the group, so the more chance of discovery.

Evelle wanted to know why Tina was at the station. She said she'd come "on business", but said nothing about the ship, about Finn, Rex or Thor. These were old high-care hospital rooms. There was usually fairly advanced surveillance equipment in those places, especially if they also treated mental patients. The pirates might be listening in. She directed the conversation away from her, asking how the ship came to be in pirate hands, and was told they had become separated from the fleet because of an intersecting asteroid cloud, and that they were ambushed by a fleet of pirate ships on the other side.

It wasn't easy to turn warships around quickly, so by the time the other ships in the fleet would have noticed the ship missing, it was too late.

Tina was familiar with the protocol. When one ship stopped communicating, you continued on to your destination and reported the matter at which time other people got to track the missing ship.

"The pirates weren't supposed to be dangerous," someone said.

There was some laughter at that.

The pirates had taken the ship to Aurora and the crew had been taken off and brought here. Twelve women were in the group. Tina asked about the rest of the crew.

"They kept us separate, men and women. We don't know where the men are."

Tina knew, but she didn't want to talk about that now. She didn't know if all the men had been taken to the dark zone to be infected with rift virus. Maybe the pirates had only done this to a few people. Maybe by now Jens had disabled the system and the cubicles had opened so that the men could wake up and hopefully walk away unharmed. From all she understood about it, the infection took longer than a few days to take hold and didn't transfer easily. Exposure to ultraviolet light was a factor.

"There are men locked up in other parts of this prison," Tina said.

"Yes, but none of them are part of the crew. We already checked that."

"Maybe they took the crew back to the ship."

"Why? We have the captain and pilots here."

"The ship is being prepared for departure," Tina said.

"How do you know that?" another woman asked.

"I saw it myself. The readiness percentage is going up."

In the darkness of the room, a female voice said, "Shit. Are you sure?"

Evelle asked, "Aliz?"

"Who are you?" Tina asked.

"Aliz Paduano. Flight Officer First Class, SF *Manila*."

"She's the first pilot," someone else said.

"I'm familiar with the language," Tina said. Then she asked Aliz, "Is there a problem?"

"Are you absolutely sure the readiness is increasing?"

"I saw it myself. I know what to look for. I used to work for the Force as biological scientist at Project Charon. I've been on many flights. It know what it looks like when a ship is being prepared for departure."

"When you saw this, was there a sign of crew on board?"

"Not that I could see."

Aliz said again, "Shit." And after a short silence, she continued, "The SF *Manila* has two reactor cores. After arrival, they need to be manually powered down before the engine can be shut down and the ship is ready to remain in dock for any length of time. Normal passenger ships with reactor cores don't have this requirement, because much of it is automated and starts without involvement from the crew, counting back from the scheduled arrival time. It's a safety issue. However, this process hampers engine output so it's unsuited to a warship like the SF *Manila*. This means that the reactor will keep burning and will start to ramp up power and readiness again, save that the ship is not actually being prepared for departure."

"That sounds nasty. What are the consequences? A lot of damage to the ship?"

"Sure, but the immediate concern is that if nothing is done, the reactor will blow up."

"Shit."

"Eeyup."

CHAPTER TWENTY-SEVEN

"SO WE'RE KIND OF SCREWED," Evelle said.

"You said it," Aliz said. "When the ship goes, it will take out the entire station."

"How long before that happens?"

"I've never tried it myself. Probably a few days."

And the *Manila* had been in dock for a few days already.

"How about we get out of here before that time?" Tina said.

"I would love to, but overwhelming the guards is very risky. We've already tried that once, when they came to bring food. Several of us got taken away. We haven't seen them since, so we're reluctant to try again without a plan because we'll still need a skeleton crew to fly the ship, and if we lose too many people we might not be able to occupy all essential positions."

Tina said, "I have some options."

"What kind of options?" Aliz sounded interested.

"Ways of getting out of here. Extra crew, maybe."

"Go on."

Tina lowered her voice. "Make a bit of noise while I'm speaking. I'm sure someone is trying to listen in."

"We've already ripped that thing out of the wall," a woman said.

Several other women had started dragging their feet over the floor which made a scuffling noise over the carpet.

The women all gathered around her.

Tina continued, "There is likely to be more than just the visible camera. I ran a business that installs and maintains security systems. Cayelle is a backwater world for many reasons, and because of that, it has a lot of crime. People buy advanced security systems. In fact, they're much more advanced than any I've seen here. I know how to disable these systems."

"That's pretty hard to do unless you have access to their computer systems."

"I have a solution for that, too." She told them about Thor, Jens and Rex without mentioning their names.

"But how would you get in contact with them?"

"I have some options. I may need some help." She explained that she wanted the women to study the walls of the room very carefully to look for panels or other ways to open the wall recess. "Keep chatting, talking about personal things, whatever."

They all spread out over the room and inspected the wall panels closely. Tina first got on her knees, starting from the ground up.

Evelle sat next to her. She said, "It's such a coincidence that this is how we meet."

"Did you ever wonder about me?"

"Sometimes. We weren't allowed to contact our families most of the time. It was very hard on some people."

"But not on you?"

She let out a sigh. "When I first joined, I was very angry. I was always facing some form of disciplinary action on board. Half the recycling plant was probably maintained by me. There's a reason I never got picked to become a pilot no matter how much I applied. It was all that stuff that went on that probably wasn't as important as I thought it was and made me angry. I was always angry."

Tina hated to think back to that time just before Evelle left home. She didn't remember all the things that were said in arguments that she had long forgotten and Evelle might remember word for word, because she had wanted to escape, for whatever unfathomable reason teenagers want that. Tina had been the same at that age: always wanting to be somewhere else, until she was somewhere else and far away when her father died.

She would have loved the opportunity to see him once more.

It was time to move on, accept the past as something that could not be changed, only forgiven. "There's no need to be angry anymore."

"But I'm sorry, Mum. I really am. I was a horrible kid."

"So was I, at that age."

"I thought I'd never see you again. I heard the stories, and then both you and Dad disappeared and no one knew where you'd gone."

In her voice, Tina could hear the little girl who had asked her to read a story, the girl who had begged her not to make her go to school. There was always trouble at the school at Project Charon. It was too small to employ enough teachers to keep track of all the students, and older kids used to do terrible things to the younger ones.

The sense of failure of their little family oozed from this

conversation. "I know this isn't the way I planned to see you, either."

"But why are you here? Have you joined them, too, like Dad?"

That was one bit Tina had suspected but didn't know for certain. "You probably know more about Dad than I do. Has he officially joined the pirates?"

"Dad was always sympathetic to them, because he said he didn't believe the Federacy Force was using the full potential of the things they discovered in space."

"We were working with it at Project Charon, but unfortunately Dexter got impatient. We weren't up to the stage where we would ever think of releasing it to the public, let alone pharmaceutical companies, and Dexter was instrumental in spreading it and enabling the pirates to take over large sections of inhabited space. They're changing the face of humanity. They're turning people into monsters with tentacles."

"I know. I've seen them. They say that it gives you great mental power and cures diseases. Other people say that while this is true, the effect is very temporary. I don't know what to believe."

"Were you doing research?" Tina asked.

"No. I'm a communications officer."

"I wonder whether Dexter is one of these monsters."

"When's the last time you saw him?"

"I spoke to him probably about eight years ago. He was complaining about having to pay for some items that he didn't agree with."

"He mentioned that to me. He said that apparently I have a brother, or at least that you were telling him he had a son. That's not really true, is it?"

"It's true. His name is Rex. He's fifteen."

"You're kidding."

"Why would I kid about that?"

"Where is he? At Cayelle?"

Tina was highly tempted to tell her about Rex, but she was also aware that the pirates were probably listening and trying to get information out of this discussion. So she said, "I'll tell you about him later."

Evelle said, "First, there's got to be a later."

"We are going to get out of here," Tina said. But she didn't know how yet.

Then someone called out, "Shhh!"

Everyone went quiet and stopped inspecting the wall.

The sound of heavy footsteps echoed on the gallery outside, as well as the voices of other prisoners in the cell next door.

A man who was nothing but a silhouette against the grey rectangle of light that came in from outside opened the door. The door was of a thick metal type that swung into the room. At the top and bottom of the frame sat a shiny metal plate with slots for bolts. Two red lights blinked in the recess that held the lock.

The man came one step into the cell. He plonked down a box, backed away and shut the door again, returning the cell to complete darkness.

"What's that?" Tina asked.

"Whatever passes for food here," Evelle said.

Several other women had already gone to the box. Someone directed a light at it, showing a box with an open top containing neatly wrapped parcels. Some type of food ration.

A woman had unwrapped one that contained a kind of

hard, dry bread. The box also held a few bottles of what appeared to be water.

"Smells funny," a woman said. She had taken the lid off one of the bottles and sniffed the top.

"I wouldn't trust that," Tina said.

"If you're thirsty, you'll drink it," someone replied.

The women were thirsty so they did drink it. Tina got a few swigs, too, before the bottle was empty and the middle-aged woman who appeared to have taken control of the distribution of food said that the other bottles would be shared later.

"Has anyone found anything of interest?" Tina asked the group.

"There's a panel next to the door," someone said.

"Probably a room control panel for light and temperature. There's likely to be a small box or recess above the door. It would be great if we could open that."

Aliz said, "Do you still have any electronics on you? Our equipment was all confiscated."

"So was mine, but I just spotted something interesting when the fellow opened the door. This area wasn't built as prison. I don't think Aurora had an official prison, because civilian stations don't tend to keep convicted criminals on-site. Too dangerous. This room is part of what used to be a hospital."

"That sounds about right," someone said. "Hospitals and prisons. Roughly the same thing, right?"

"This room was probably a private room for infectious or difficult patients and there would have been a camera, which you said you already ripped out of the wall. If none of us have found any additional panels, that points to an older system, which would fit with the rest of the station. This was only a hospital after all. No need for huge security investments. I'd hoped to find a second camera."

"I have the old one in my pocket. Would that help you?"

"No. I'm after the control box that would be associated with it. With the older system, I'll need to get into the one that's associated with the control panel, and there's a greater risk of accidentally doing something stupid. Anyway, that's not to be helped. The box is probably above the door. I've installed a lot of those systems. Give me a leg up."

Tina took off her boots and stepped into the linked hands of someone, probably Evelle. She heaved herself up and ran her hands over the wall above the door and the nearby ceiling.

After a while, Evelle said, "Oof, you're heavy. I'm going to have to put you down."

"Are you calling me fat?" But she jumped down. Evelle was slight, and Tina had the build of a middle-aged woman. "I better lift you instead."

"Okay. What am I looking for?"

"A panel that can open or anything that feels like it's not part of the wall."

Evelle stepped into Tina's linked hands and moved around, feeling the wall as far as she could reach. "I don't feel anything. What if they put it somewhere else in the room?"

"Then they're stupid. You put the camera over the door, because when people walk through the door, they always face the same way. It's your best chance to get a look at their face. If you're only going to have one control box, you put it next to the camera."

"Sheesh, of course," someone else said.

Then Evelle said, "I think I have something. There's a smooth panel here."

"Can you find a groove or screws?"

"Not really."

"Let me have a look."

A reshuffle ensued, where Evelle used another woman's hands and a few more women helped Tina up. She ran her hands along the smooth wall until they met Evelle's.

"You have cold hands."

"Sorry."

Tina found the panel. The edges were slightly elevated above the metal of the wall. There was no groove between the wall and the panel. Yet there had to be some way to service the equipment. She pushed on the panel. It moved into the wall and sprang back to its original position.

Ah.

Now she pushed two corners with both hands at the same time. The panel popped out of the wall. She handed the cover down to the women who stood there.

Inside the panel she found wires neatly bunched together and tied with a clip. She'd need some light to see which ones she could cut.

There was also a small display, which lit up when she touched it.

Now they were getting somewhere.

CHAPTER TWENTY-EIGHT

TINA JUMPED TO THE GROUND.

"Before I touch that computer, we need to have a plan for what we're going to do. As soon as I start fiddling with the wiring and sending people messages, they'll know we've broken in and they'll be over here in no time. We have a very short time frame to get out of here, warn my people off-site that we're coming, and find a safe place to hide. Do you know anything about the likely situation we'll face in the area around this room?"

Evelle replied, "When we came here, it was from the ground floor. To the anti-spinward direction an exit leads to a corridor that goes to the docks."

That was different than the way Tina had come in, but likely the way through the agriculture sector was quicker. Of course the pirates had avoided taking prisoners through the labs.

She described, as best as she could, the layout of the rest of the station as she remembered from the map.

It was hard to do this without visuals, but one woman called

Margot, who was a cook, proposed to allocate letters to the chambers that Tina described. They worked through chambers A—the old hospital—to the lab which was B and the recycling plant which was C and then the agriculture plant which was D. Talking about spinward and anti-spinward was second nature to people having grown up in space, but Tina hadn't, and she had forgotten how subtle hints in how things moved and weight shifted told the inhabitants which was which.

She led the group on a virtual tour of the route to the docks twice. She asked if they knew how to find the ship and, as it turned out, Aliz was one of an experimental generation of pilots who were awarded their position for the duration of their careers and carried an implant that linked them with the ship.

"It doesn't work in here, of course. The silence in my head drives me nuts, but once I'm close enough nothing will stop the ship showing me how to reach it. And I need to get back to the ship as soon as possible."

Tina asked, "Do you think you can stabilise the ship enough that we can use it, or do we try to get out some other way?" Although that might be hard, because as far as she knew, the docks were still closed, and there might not be time to wait for the *Alethia* to come in. Tina didn't think they'd all fit aboard her ship, anyway.

"I don't have a choice," Aliz said. "I either stabilise the ship or die. I would love to have at least one engineer."

And Finn, of course, was not at the station.

"I may be able to get someone who is pretty good at maintenance," Tina said. Although this ship was likely to be far out of Thor's experience and capability.

Aliz said the first concern was that they had to take the

Manila out of dock. Some repairs could only be done in zero gravity. If there was extensive damage, they might have to wait for Federacy engineers to turn up, but that was a worry for later. An added problem was that everyone who had been in the departure queue had just plundered all the ship's rations. How many people would they be able to take?

Another problem was that the ship was likely to be guarded. No one had weapons. They could try to overwhelm some guards and steal their weapons. They agreed that was messy and to be avoided.

Or they could create a diversion and hope that the pirates would be too undisciplined to keep an eye on them.

"They only look stupid," Evelle said. "They aren't stupid at all."

Tina agreed. "We shouldn't underestimate them, especially not the mutants. They can flick those tentacles across the room and can hear what you say from a long distance off. There's also some indication that they're resistant to low-level laser weapons."

Aliz said, "I wouldn't want to use a Q-blaster inside a station. That's going to blow a hole in the hull."

"We'd need smarter weapons," someone said.

Evelle said, "No. We need knives or something to harm them physically."

"Bows and arrows," someone else said.

That triggered a cascade of ideas. The mutant pirates might not be susceptible to laser weapons, but they wouldn't have the same protection against physical weapons. No one was going to shoot bullets inside a space station either, and no one should get too close to the mutant pirates, but spears and knives might keep them occupied for long enough that the women could escape. And arrows. Where would they get those kinds of weapons?

Then Tina remembered Jens and his catapult. That was a perfect weapon. It wasn't going to injure or kill anyone, but it would distract them. "Does anyone have any elastic?"

It went quiet for a moment.

Margot asked, "What do you want that for?"

"I have an idea. See if you can find elastic. I'm going to see what else I can find."

Tina climbed back up to the open panel. With a lot of yanking, she managed to take another panel off. The space underneath was filled with wires, many of them inside insulation tubes. It took three women to pull loose a couple of the tubes. Tina hoped that the wires they disturbed didn't trigger any warnings.

The tubes were made of tough plastic with a foam insulation inside. Tina managed to snap one in half, and tied the resulting two segments in a cross with a piece of wire. By this time, someone handed her a slightly stretchy length of fabric.

"What's this?"

"Tights. It's all we have in the way of elastic."

That wasn't going to do the job. She explained she needed something more robust than that.

Evelle said, "The door seal."

That was an excellent idea, but they could only get it out when the door was open, and at that time they needed to hurry.

That meant first they would need to provide everyone with a weapon of some sort, even if it was only a stick, and would need to find objects to pass as ammunition for the catapult.

Tina opened another panel, which opened the wall down to the floor of the room. They ran out of tubing that they could pull out, but a metal strut came loose, and builders had left a box of unused rivets in the wall space. They were about the length of her thumb, with a blunt end and a sharp end. Tina gave each of the women a hand full and put the rest of the box in her pocket.

With all the rummaging they had done inside the wall space, and the cables they had untied, the security control screen was now hanging at shoulder height.

Tina went to the door and listened. The gallery space on the other side with four floors of prison cells was quiet except for the occasional knocking or a muffled voice inside one of the other rooms. "Do you know where the guards normally sit?"

"They tend to walk around a lot," Evelle said. "Mostly on the ground floor. You can hear them talk to each other."

The fact that there were no guards patrolling the gallery probably meant some sort of electronic system was in place. Those systems usually relied on the heat of bodies to check for the presence of people. Movement sensors was another possibility, but they only operated at close range, while infrared systems could see at a much greater distance. On top of that, someone was likely to monitor the prison from a remote room. They would turn up at the slightest indication of trouble.

It was time for action.

Tina explained what she was going to do and what the members of the group should do once the door was open. "I'll contact my friends when we're ready. It's quite likely that whatever they do will open all the locks of the surrounding rooms as well, so there will be chaos outside. It's our focus to get out of here to the SF *Manila*. As soon as the door is open, we'll pull out the door seal and cut it into lengths to make as many slingshots as possible. Use the rivets as ammunition if necessary.

Pick up anything else we can use as ammunition. Aim for areas where it's going to be annoying. Their faces would be good, or if you can, damage their equipment. Take their weapons if you can get them, but don't fire them."

Aliz said, "For now, until we get back to a Federacy ship or base, your usual rank and command structure is dissolved. You will take orders from Tina, with myself and Evelle as second in command."

"Understood," someone said, and others agreed.

Tina continued, "We'll make for the docks via the shortest route. Don't get distracted by what you see, because you will see disturbing things." She was going to have to take them through the labs. "Don't get distracted thinking you might be able to help crewmembers. We might be able to help them, but not if we don't succeed in getting out ourselves first."

The women accepted that.

Aliz then spoke about what they needed to do first when they arrived at the ship. "I'm going to have to turn up the engine as much as possible without triggering warnings about overheating of the engine chambers. The ship needs to shed power as quickly as possible. Preferably without frying anything important."

She assigned some tasks which the crewmembers understood.

A couple of women had questions about what to do when they encountered resistance.

Aliz said, "Don't engage. Don't fight to win, even if we're attacked. Fight only if they block our route to escape."

Tina went again through the basic layout of the station so that they could find their own way in case they were separated or the way ahead was blocked. She told them about the passages that Jens had used to enter the sector illegally.

The message was simple: get to the ship. If people got caught and left behind, keep going. The ship would leave when there was an essential crew on board. The Federacy Force would come back later.

Only one thing was left to do: contact Rex and Jens and get them to disable as much of the security system in this sector as possible. And tell them to keep quiet and then contact Finn to pick them up once the docks were open again.

She might not see Rex for a long time.

Tina activated the screen.

CHAPTER TWENTY-NINE

TINA USED JENS' instructions to access the station's general system and quickly navigated through the menus. She sent a message to Thor, asking him to disable as many security systems as possible. He replied that he had read the message.

A moment later, a loud click sounded inside the door. Evelle pushed it. It opened.

"Quick, let's go," Tina called out.

First Evelle pulled the inner door seal from the frame. It was nice, springy rubber, soft and stretchy. Evelle cut it into pieces by running it over the sharp edge of the doorframe with the door ajar. Tina tied a length to the two pieces of tubing and tested the slingshot with her fingers. It would have to do.

She gave it to Margot and made two more of these makeshift weapons.

They were out of time and really needed to start moving.

They walked in single file along the gallery. Tina couldn't see anyone at the ground level of the atrium, but that wouldn't last very long.

Women banged on the cell doors they passed. "Get out. Door's open! Get out, get out!"

The men came out of their cells. Some were bewildered, some ran, some shouted. Some could barely walk, and squinted against what little light entered the atrium. How long had they been inside the dark room?

It got quite crowded on the gallery.

"Do you see any of the crew members?" Tina asked Evelle.

"I don't see anyone familiar."

Tina was disturbed by how much of Dexter she could see in Evelle. Much more than Rex.

Despite having been locked up with them, Tina hadn't seen most of the ship's crew yet. Aliz turned out to be a middle-aged woman with greying hair. Margot was younger, with very pretty eyes and velvet black skin. Evelle looked pale. Her bruise had gone yellow.

Everyone hurried for the stairs. Tina made sure not to lose the others in the press of unwashed bodies.

Prisoners were already streaming across the ground floor of the atrium, where the few makeshift guards were struggling to contain them. Their computer systems were down. Tina could see the warnings flash over their screens. The guards were split between re-establishing communication with their supervisors and stopping the prisoners escaping. The flood of prisoners coming down the stairs was too big for the few men to handle.

They were panicked and clearly poorly trained.

Panicked guards did stupid things, especially if they had weapons.

"Hey," a male voice said next to Tina.

She turned around and recognised the father from the

blue shipworld family she had defended against a bully in the *Manila*'s galley. What was he doing here?

"Are they locking up their own people now?" she asked.

"We're not their people. They took our name and destroyed it. They came to us and thought they could get away with thuggery. They saw we had no leader and thought we needed one. And those who protested, they locked up."

"You're free to go now."

"We won't rest until we expel this menace from our world."

Other men agreed.

She lost contact with him in the throng of people pushing through the narrow alleys. It was hard enough keeping up with Evelle and the other women.

The stream of prisoners went through a doorway on the other side of the hall, held open because someone had jammed a piece of metal in between the door and the doorframe.

That was the passage where most of them would have entered the hospital that served as a prison.

Tina knew that the hospital was next to the huge experiment room. She also knew that there was a door between the two, at the lowest level.

Instead of making for the passage where everyone else was going, she led the group to the far end of the atrium, underneath the overhanging gallery. It was dark and dusty down there. Light from the atrium's ceiling barely reached the far corner of what looked like a haphazard storage space.

A panel to the side of a set of double doors at the far end blinked with green lights: the doors were operational and unlocked.

Tina waited until everyone in the group had caught up.

Shouting voices echoed elsewhere in the hall. It sounded like reinforcements had arrived. Time was short.

She held the door open while all the crew members filed into a connecting hallway.

Tina made sure that the door shut behind them, but some people had already followed, a bunch of men who looked like independent merchants. That was not to be helped.

She ran after the others, but they had stopped at an open door. Over their heads, Tina could see the many shelves of the lab room, all of them in semidarkness.

"What's going on? Hurry up, we don't have all day," called a woman in front of her.

"Are you sure it's safe to go through here?" Evelle asked.

"Go," Tina said.

"The boss says to keep going!"

Tina pushed between the people at the front of the group. They were all standing a few steps into the door of the large experimental room, staring at the shelves of cabinets.

"There's people in here," Margot said, her voice disturbed.

"Whoa, they're trying to make them better?" a woman asked.

It was hard to see anything. The blue light inside the cabinets was off. Control panels flashed with red or orange lights. Jens had done a very good job of disabling power.

She took the lead, running along the centre aisle through the hall.

With all the blue light gone, it was very dark and she had to be careful not to trip over anything.

They were almost through the hall when she spotted a silhouette on the lowest gallery.

"Careful," she whispered to Evelle behind her. "There's someone up there."

"Where?"

Tina pointed at the man silhouetted against the light from an emergency exit. He walked awkwardly as if his legs weren't working properly.

"Who are you?" Aliz asked.

A male voice made a gurgling sound and then coughed.

A woman said, "Vito?"

The only reply was more coughing.

The man stumbled down the stairs, where someone directed a light from the emergency lamp on his face.

The man looked pale, thin and his clothes were all wet with a slimy substance. His eyes were unfocused and he was shivering.

"Vito! It's me, Miriam!"

He didn't react to her.

"Quick, give him a blanket."

"Look, there are some others. Gerry and Stan."

Those men were just coming down the stairs. They, too, were wet and their expressions were distant.

Tina ran up the stairs.

Several of the cabinets where the men had been asleep had been vandalised. Broken glass lay on the ground, the lid was open and the control panel flashed red lights.

Wait—the glass had sprayed outwards on this one. That meant the cabinet had been opened from the inside.

Tina could only guess what had happened: the man had woken up because of the power failure and had smashed the cover from inside before helping others.

The women discovered eight crewmembers amongst the men. The others were merchants or pirates or travellers, or maybe people from the station, but their Sinolese was hard to understand.

It was hard not to stop and help them all, but they had to keep going.

Aliz and some of the other women helped the men who were unsteady on their feet. They didn't say much, the empty expressions disturbing.

"Come on, walk as quickly as possible,' Tina said.

The pirates would be on the lookout for the source of the trouble and she didn't yet know how hard it would be to get through the checkpoint at the end of the agriculture sector.

They walked through the recycling plant and the agriculture hall. Whatever Jens had done had also disabled the banks of lights that hung over the plants. Only sporadic lights on the outer edges of the gallery illuminated the central aisle. Just as well it was wide and uncluttered.

Ahead Tina could already see the checkpoint.

With the men from the crew still shivering and weak, they walked slowly. A few people caught up with them. These were Freeranger pirates in their shipworld's dress.

Tina couldn't see the blue ones anywhere. The most prevalent ones were a group in mustard-coloured dress. They even had children with them.

From a distance, Tina spotted at least four guards at the checkpoint into the docks. A number of people also stood on the other side. One of the guards called out.

Someone behind her replied.

Damn, a group of pirates had come up from behind. Tina could hear voices and footsteps approaching through the dark hall.

The pirates at the checkpoint sprang into alertness.

"We're caught between the two," Evelle said. "They don't know we're here."

"To the side," Tina said, as loudly as she dared. "Hide."

The group ducked into a side passage between two tables full of plants. It was extremely dark in here. Tina told all of them to sit on the floor. Several of the women helped the men. They were still dazed and none of them had spoken a word. What had the pirates done to them in those cabinets?

A moment later, a group of people strode past at a rather fast pace. From where Tina sat, she only saw them as silhouettes against the faint glow from a light on the other side of the aisle. Their voices carried through the empty hall. One of them sounded familiar, a woman's voice.

At least ten men with the stout build of mutants accompanied her. In between the wall of mutant men, she spotted the figure of a slender woman. The group went in the direction of the checkpoint, out of Tina's view.

The men at the checkpoint yelled for people to stand aside. This woman must be important. What was the bet that this was the station director?

Maybe she had an office in the agriculture sector and had been caught out by the power outage?

Tina had an idea how to get past those guards. She was still wearing the borrowed station overalls and could pass for a maintenance officer.

"Everyone pick up a box that looks like we're moving stuff," she said.

Shelves lined the walls, containing boxes of parts for the irrigation system, tools or sampling equipment. She found a number of transport boxes and handed them out to members of the group. She even found some lab overalls, which she handed to the men, who needed assistance putting them on.

Aliz said, "What are we doing? There are just tube connectors in this box."

"We pretend we're moving stuff, just to get past the check point. Everyone ready?"

But at this point, another, much bigger, group of people came from behind and walked through the aisle. The voices of those people sounded angry.

"Who are you? How did you get in here?" Tina could hear one of the guards at the checkpoint ask them.

The reply got lost in angry shouts, and an argument broke out.

At one point, a man called, "We don't give out passes. You have to apply to station management."

And then, a bit later, "I know the power is out. We're working on it! Just have some patience."

And then, "Wait. Who says you can go through?"

Another male voice called into the hall, "We could use some assistance here!"

Tina got up, peeping over the benches with plants. People were streaming through the checkpoint, while the guards tried to stop them, but they were too few.

"Let's go." She picked up a transport crate and waited for the others to do the same.

Hopefully the guards would be too busy to pay much attention to them.

Tina led the way back into the aisle, checking over her shoulder to see if the others followed. Evelle walked behind her, carrying a box, but several other women had to support the men who couldn't walk unaided. Two men seemed to have recovered, which was a hopeful sign.

The large group of people was still at the checkpoint and the argument over whether they could proceed continued.

Tina led the group to the side, where a sign proclaimed, *Authorised Entry*.

"What are you up to?" a guard asked Tina.

"The boss asked us to bring this stuff for her." Referring to the station director coming past.

The guard eyed her and her group suspiciously.

They didn't exactly look like guard material. The men might be wearing lab overalls, but none of them were the correct size. Some of the men still had wet hair, and all of them retained that distant look in their eyes.

The women looked—and smelled—like they had spent time in prison.

Tina could see conflicting thoughts whirl in his eyes. Were she and her group worth creating more trouble, while his mates were already dealing with the other, much larger, group? All of those people were Freeranger pirates, supposedly allies, but one elderly man in the group had the guards holed up and was shouting at them.

Several of the younger men—the old man's sons?—crowded around a guard.

The man nodded at Tina to proceed.

CHAPTER THIRTY

PHEW.

Tina was glad for the break and hoped they could get far enough away before the guards discovered that they'd let through their prize escapees.

But they were now in the docks area, close to the *Manila*.

This area still had power, but a sense of heightened vigilance hung in the air. Heavily armed pirates stood at intervals. People in station overalls sped through the passages. Their expressions were serious. No one was chatting.

Tina ducked into the first control niche she could find, typed the passcode Jens had given her into the computer and tried to contact the apartment.

We've escaped. In the docks. Contact Finn.

But Jens didn't reply.

Tina waited, her heart thudding. What had happened?

"What is it?" Evelle asked.

"Your brother. I hoped he could come here."

But the docks were still officially closed. Time was ticking for the *Manila*'s critical failure clock.

They needed to keep moving.

A few of the men were visibly weakening. It wouldn't be possible to make a run for it with this group, or get involved in a fight.

"We need to go to the ship as soon as possible," Aliz said, her voice rough with urgency. She held her hand to the side of her head, as if the feed she was getting from the ship was so noisy that she could barely hear what went on around her. "If it's not too late already."

"How about you go with a few crew members to help you?" Tina said.

"Once we're at the ship, we're going to leave with it immediately," Aliz said. "I need to shed power and can't do that while moored."

"I know. I have to find my son and our friends. They haven't responded to my messages."

She had not received a confirmation, only one that the message had been read.

"I could really use you," Aliz said. "I don't have anyone else with flying experience, no matter how unrelated."

"Mum, please?"

Tina met Evelle's eyes.

She was strong, independent, and Tina saw a younger version of herself in her. Desperate to escape, and to be happy. Did Evelle have a partner? Did she think about her scattered family during her daily routines?

Out of the group of women, Aliz and Evelle were the most technically competent in terms of operating the ship. Evelle wasn't even a pilot.

She couldn't leave them alone.

But Rex needed her. Didn't he?

Rex had been independent for the last few months, ever

since getting his new harness. He was with Thor and Jens, and those two would be smart enough to keep their heads down. Besides, Rex had Finn and Rasa to collect the three of them off the station. Rex had good companions, his own quasi-family. Evelle needed her more than he did.

She nodded. "Let's go."

But while they made their way through the passages, Tina kept looking over her shoulders, just in case Thor, Rex and Jens turned up.

They didn't.

It was surprisingly busy in the docks. She caught shards of conversations about the power outage that had brought down many of the systems the pirates used to guard the area.

Were the docks still closed to incoming or outgoing ships? It didn't look like it. There were too many people around.

Aliz led the way, her expression haunted. Now that they were close to the ship, she could communicate with it again.

"The ship is in distress," she said. "Systems are critical. We need to hurry. We have fifteen minutes to major failure."

"Run ahead," Tina said. "Start whatever procedure needs starting. We'll catch up."

They came into the lift foyer where Tina had first seen Evelle. The room was packed. What were all these people doing here?

They were all facing the lift doors. The station director stood there, dressed in ship overalls, wearing an earpiece microphone. Her voice carried through the hall but she spoke in Sinolese and Tina understood none of it.

Every now and then the people cheered and clapped.

"The selfish bitch," Aliz said.

"What is she talking about?" Tina asked.

"She's talking about how she's going to ask her friends for

help," Evelle said and then frowned at Tina. "You don't know Sinolese?"

"I hated learning it so much at school that I've forgotten all of it. I never used it anyway."

"Screw asking friends for help," Aliz said. "She knows the Federacy Force is underway and as a pirate supporter she has no chance of escape once they're here."

"Look over there," Evelle said.

Tina looked where she was pointing. A couple of screens displayed the status of a long list of ships in dock. They had strange names like *Futility Notwithstanding* and *Only Joking* and many of them were shown as *loading*.

Pirate ships.

"Do you think they're vacating the station?" Tina asked. Was that what this dock closure was about?

"No, that's not what I mean. Look," Evelle said.

The list on one of the screens had changed. These were cargo ships, mostly idling in dock at fifteen to twenty percent readiness.

Except one line said, "SF *Manila*. Readiness one hundred and five percent."

"We have to hurry," Aliz said.

But how? There were too many people in this hall. They needed to cross the hall, and now something was happening: a group of pirate guards came out of the same passage where Evelle and the other crew from the *Manila* had been led away. They were followed by a group of people.

They were all men. They were dressed in the same grey station suits. Each one had a number painted on their chest pocket.

The men all wore the same blank expression. They were human, but several showed mottled patches on their skin.

They marched in neat formation across the hall over a path cleared by the pirate guards. The lift doors opened and about twenty of them went in.

Loading.

What was the bet that this was the cargo being loaded? Mindless soldiers. Cannon fodder being sent off to war?

And all this was happening while the *Manila* was getting dangerously overheated, a time bomb ticking inexorably towards a catastrophic ending. Why had no one properly disengaged the engines? Was this done on purpose? Were the pirates unable to stop the process?

Then Margot said, "No." She stared, horrified, at another group of prisoners being led into the hall.

"Those are *Manila* crew," Evelle said.

The men all still had healthy skin, but their eyes held an eerily distant expression.

"They've been sedated," Evelle said.

"That's disgusting," Aliz said.

Next to Tina, two women struggled to hold back one of the male crewmembers they had rescued. His face was sweaty and he opened and closed his mouth as if he wanted to call out, but no sound came out.

He yanked himself free from the women and lunged to the path through the crowd. A pirate soldier stood there and noticed the attack from within the crowd too late.

The crewmember grabbed hold of the pirate's weapon, a Fireseed model. Before the pirate could react, he had pulled the weapon free, turned it on, aimed and—

"No, don't!" Tina called out.

But it was already too late.

The crackling beam hit the pirate. He froze. A shudder went through his body. He stood there, with a surprised expression on his face, for what seemed like a long time. And then a volley of crackling lightning beams flew from his skin, hitting bystanders. People screamed and tried to run away, but there was nowhere to run.

In the throng of panicked people, Tina was pushed against the people behind her, who themselves were pushed against the wall.

The crackling light also hit other mutant pirates, who spread the lightning further through the hall, to other people and other pirates.

Pandemonium broke out in the hall. People tried to make for the couple of escape routes. The lift, the passage to the right, the passage across from where Tina stood that led into the docks.

The pirate guards formed a wall around the station director.

Tina was left with Evelle, Aliz and Margot, two other women and two rescued men. The man who had fired the gun wasn't one of them. That man was likely to have been swooped on by pirates.

One of the women had been hit, and she clutched her arm.

"Come on, we have to go," Aliz said. "We need to get to the ship."

The dock status screen cycled through the list of docked ships, oblivious to the panic, showing the *Manila* at one hundred and six percent readiness.

Another load of new soldiers had arrived upon the chaos. They stood bunched together in a group, with the pirate at the front looking visibly bewildered on how he was going to get to the lift.

Onlookers were shouting at the new soldiers. Many of

those men only displayed the beginnings of mottled skin, and they retained their human features.

The pirate guard frantically tried to keep the onlookers away, but several people from the crowd were trying to pull the soldiers out of their formation. Tina guessed these men were some of the missing locals.

"We can't get out!" Aliz called over the yelling and shouting.

Her eyes were wide, her face pale and sheened with sweat. Tina couldn't imagine what it was like to be paired with a ship and feel its distress.

"This way!" Evelle led them through the crowd.

They dodged fistfights, arguments, jostlings. But at the exit that led to the *Manila*'s position stood a group of pirates.

Tina stuck her hand in the pocket of her jacket and grabbed a couple of rivets. She put most of them in her breast pocket, but kept one, placing it against the elastic of the door seal catapult. She pulled.

And pulled and pulled as hard as the could.

Then she released the elastic.

The rivet flew over the heads of the crowd. It missed a pirate's shoulder by a hair's width and hit the metal wall next to him with a sharp *thwack*.

The man turned around, presumably saw the projectile, and shouted, pointing across the crowd, roughly in Tina's direction.

Tina pulled out another rivet. This time, she aimed for the light in the ceiling.

The rivet hit the light cover with a thwack that was audible over the shouting. The light shattered, spraying shards of glass everywhere.

Then she aimed at the lift panel and broke the screen with a shower of sparks.

Next to her, Margot was doing the same, hitting a pirate guard in the face. He searched the crowd for the origin of the projectile.

The crowd surged back and forth.

A man who looked like a private merchant yelled, "Let us go to our ships."

"Yeah. No reason to keep us here."

Zia Partlow was wrestling with the wrecked lift screen, trying to punch it back into action.

Tina led her group of women through the chaos. In the throng of the crowd, Evelle took her hand. Tina squeezed it. They were going to get through this together.

The merchants and other visitors to the station ganged up on the pirates, demanding access to their ships.

It was strange how so many people had managed to stay at the station, when she knew for a fact that all the ships had been told to leave. It didn't make any sense.

Then a thought: what if Thor had sent these people? They were no merchants. They were locals helping her out by creating a ruckus. Whether or not this was intentional, the effect was that they had drawn all the pirate guards into this hall.

"We need to go. We need to go or we'll all die." Aliz's face was pale.

"I'm working on it," Tina said.

"No you don't understand. We need to go now."

Three guards stood at the entrance to the passage to the docks. Unlike the other guards, they were not involved in any arguments.

Tina aimed a rivet with her catapult, but it missed.

Aliz pushed past her. "We need to go now."

"Wait." Tina pulled her jacket, but Aliz kept going.

"We have to go now." Her eyes were wide.

Before Tina could stop her, Aliz marched up to the guards. She didn't even talk to them, but tried to sneak between them.

"Hey, where do you think you're going?"

Aliz turned around. She hefted the length of tubing over her head and brought it down on the pirate's head with such force that the casing shattered. Bits of insulation foam flew everywhere. The man crumpled.

There was nothing for it.

Too close to the pirates to hit out, Tina thrust her catapult forward, poking a second pirate in the eye.

Evelle shoved the third man into the wall with such force that Tina could feel the thud as his head hit the metal.

"Run!" Evelle shouted.

They ran. Aliz first and then Tina and Evelle, followed by Margot and the remaining two women and two men.

Around the corner, and then through a corridor until they reached the position of the *Manila*.

The screen next to the door said one hundred and eight percent readiness. The letters on the display flashed.

"Come on," Aliz said. "Hurry up, hurry up!"

Tina ran inside following Aliz, turned right and almost tripped over some piece of clothing left there from the fight. An alarm blared inside the ship's corridors.

"Shut the doors, secure the hatch!" Evelle called over her shoulder.

Up the stairs.

The set of screens in the landing was flashing warnings. Overheating. Irreversible damage imminent.

Tina followed Aliz onto the bridge.

Aliz jumped into the main pilot seat, yanked on her earpiece, and flicked levers up and down. Her lips moved. "Go, go, go, baby, go." And then to Station Control, "No, I'm not waiting for permission to leave. This is an emergency. Tina! Get the maps, get the navigation module online. Plot us a path that gets us out quickly and isn't going to put us on a collision course with anything major."

Tina scrambled to find these things. This ship was so big, everything was strange for her, and in places she didn't expect it to be. The *Alethia* had a navigation post, but this one was huge, with several control panels and screens. She located a map of the ship's immediate surroundings. They were clear on one side, but the access tube hadn't yet disconnected fully, even if the airlocks were shut.

Tina said, "I don't know how to disengage the tube. The station needs to do it."

Evelle said, "Maybe I can—"

Aliz waved her hand, "Take the second officer's station. I'm declassifying all ship operations. Log into Jackson's account."

Evelle took the seat and strapped herself in.

A row of lights on the panel lit up in red. An alarm started blaring.

"Shut that off. Check on core function."

"Overheating."

"Time to critical."

"Four minutes, twenty-six seconds."

"Status LEC."

"Ready."

"REC."

"Warning. Overheating."

"LEA."

"Ready."

So they continued on for what seemed like a long time.

Tina flicked through the maps, finding the navigation plotting input and planning an escape route. The warning about the access tube would not go away. There were no station workers to disengage the tube.

Then Aliz said, "All systems ready, or as ready as we're going to get. Hang on. This is going to be a wild ride."

Tina said, "The access tube—"

"Tough luck. That's their problem."

She flicked another switch. "Flight Officer Paduano to crew: secure yourself at your stations. Departure imminent."

She placed her hand on the main engine control and pushed it up. The floor hummed with power.

Something creaked and hit the outside of the hull with a snap. The access tube.

She pushed up the engine control further.

The ship lurched. They shot forward. Tina was pressed into her seat and the pressure increased and increased as the ship jumped forward and zigzagged. Loose objects flew through the cabin. On the screen before her, she could follow the ship taking the course she had plotted.

They were free of the station.

CHAPTER THIRTY-ONE

OVER THE NEXT ten minutes or so, the red flashing warnings on the controls stopped flashing one by one. Aliz pulled back on the engine output and put the main engine on autopilot. Gradually, a sense of calm returned to the bridge.

Phew.

"That was one of the most ridiculous things I've ever done," Aliz said. "I'm going to be severely disciplined."

"That would be unfair. You prevented much worse," Tina said.

"That's not how those people think. I risked the ship and left port with much less than a minimum crew. I disobeyed station control. I damaged station structures. Lives may have been lost because of it."

Tina knew that she was right about all of these things. If someone was upset—and they would be, even if only for the fact that the ship had been captured at all—they would find a way to assign blame or dole out punishment, or both. Besides, loyalty to the crew was drummed into new recruits from the moment they signed up, and the ship had left the majority of its crew behind.

"We're not out of trouble yet," Aliz said. "We're extremely sparsely crewed. There is no one on board I'd trust unconditionally with the captain's chair and obviously I'm going to have to sleep. No engineers. We're likely to have a couple of high-care passengers. We're not in a safe area yet. I don't know if we have enough reserves to get to a safe area."

"If the ship has a mid-space docking facility, I can get an engineer." She told Aliz about Finn.

Her eyes widened. "Really, a Kaspari? From the Olympus Kaspari family?"

"The very one. He has some emotional baggage, but he used to be a core shield engineer on the SS *Stavanger*."

"I can use him. We have an internal dock. It's normally used for dragon fighters, but we lost most of those when we were captured. Evelle can figure out how to rearrange the shelving so it can accommodate your ship. We need to get that engineer on board."

Tina then told Evelle about the things they had set up with Thor and Jens.

"I like the way you work," Evelle said. "Lots of backup and redundancy. I'm sure we'll be able to contact that ship."

Aliz then sent Tina to locate and check on the other people on board, and report on the state they were in.

It was safe enough to move about the cabin, so Tina disconnected herself from the chair and floated through the cabin. As a front-line attack warship, the *Manila* didn't waste energy with such fripperies as a revolving habitat, even if it also meant the crew spent a significant part of their time in the gym. Being in the gym was better than doing nothing, and revolving habitats were vulnerable to space rock strikes and radiation, not to mention enemy attack.

The ship was so underoccupied that it was hard to find the other crewmembers. Tina pulled herself through passages, listening for voices.

Many things had come loose during their departure from the station, and some of the mishaps had resulted in minor damage. A tool kit floated in one of the passages, having knocked a neatly hammer-shaped dent in the wall during one of the ship's manoeuvres.

Some crew cabins had been left open and unsecured, and the bedding had migrated to block the air intake vent in the passage. Tina tried to pull it loose, but the blanket had been sucked into the fan and was hopelessly entangled.

With every passage she traversed, it became clearer that they needed more people to run the ship safely. A lot more people. Was there an option to quarantine part of the ship and run it like a much smaller vessel? There might be, but certainly Aliz would have activated that option already if it existed?

Tina finally found the rest of the ship's occupants in one of the mess rooms, a small sorry huddle of people, several of them injured, lost in the huge space with many empty "food stations" set on a frame of bars that crossed the space at regular intervals. They were probably struts that added to the structural toughness of the ship. In these warships, nothing was ever purely there for comfort.

The small group had secured themselves against the wall. Tina was happy to see Margot with the group.

"We were wondering who ended up making it on board. I was hoping you were here." The bright look on Margot's face was the first happiness Tina saw.

With Margot were a handful of other women and three of the rescued men.

During their sudden departure, several people had been unsecured and had been thrown about. One of the men had an ugly bruise on his forehead. He held his arm in a strange position, even if he didn't complain about pain, and remained eerily unresponsive to Tina's question.

One of the women was extremely concerned about people who had been left behind. "We have to go back to get them," she said.

Tina didn't say that she didn't think the ship was going anywhere in a hurry. She just hoped that Federacy reinforcements would get to the system before the pirates could recapture the ship. They were vulnerable.

The members of the group were cold, hungry and miserable. Tina said she'd see what she could do about food and turning up the temperature. She suspected they would close off parts of the ship and only occupy sections near the bridge.

These ships had rules about only essential crew being allowed on the bridge, and Tina didn't want to break that rule without the pilot's permission, so she went to report to Aliz.

"We have a total of sixteen people on board, including us. Two of the women from the prison cell got left behind. We still have three men on board, but although they can move and seem to listen, they haven't communicated that they're able to do their jobs."

Even while Tina was speaking, Evelle shook her head.

Then Aliz confirmed that sentiment. "I'm not willing to take this ship across deep space with so few resources. I need at least another pilot and an engineer, a navigator and three capable people to monitor the ship's vitals. At the very minimum. I would love to have a third pilot, especially one who is licensed for dragon fighters. We still have a couple."

"We'll have an engineer when Finn comes on board," Tina said.

But Finn wasn't responding and was probably keeping his head down in the wake of the disruptions.

Meanwhile, the *Manila* wasn't going anywhere.

Aurora Station's news channel was very vague about the happenings. Apparently, when the *Manila* ripped out the access tube, pressure had been lost in a section of the docks, and a number of pirates had been sucked into space.

It worried Tina that they had no news from Finn. Evelle scanned the cloud of merchant vessels waiting a short distance from the station, but couldn't find the ship, although that could be because Aliz didn't allow her to turn on the strongest transmitters.

"Let the station think we're dead. Those friends of yours know where we are, right?"

Tina said that she thought so, but it frustrated her that the *Alethia* wasn't out here waiting for them. This wasn't working out the way she had hoped.

But Evelle touched her on the shoulder.

"Hey, we're family," she said. "They'll find us."

"I thought you didn't care about family," Tina said.

Evelle shrugged. "I used to play tough and say I didn't miss being part of a family. Most of the time, I don't."

"But?"

"About a year ago, I was pretty sick for a few weeks. I couldn't work and I was bored in the hospital ship. I was reading a lot of things, and I came across something about Dad. It didn't say anything I didn't already know, but it said that no one knew what had happened to him, and then I thought about when I wanted you to wish me a happy birthday when I turned twenty, and I sent you a message but it was returned because Project Charon didn't exist anymore, and no one knew where you had gone." Her voice was soft. "At that moment I believed I was all alone and no one would care if I died." Her voice sounded insecure.

"But I care," Tina said. "Rex cares."

Evelle nodded. She was in ship uniform, a set of grey overalls with the name of the ship on the breast pocket. She looked tough, but Tina didn't miss the glint in her eye.

She said in a low voice. "I'm afraid Dad may have been set up. I'd give up my position to know what happened to him."

———

THE STORY CONTINUES in book 3, Survival Mode, in which Tina, Evelle and the crew battle to keep the ship and its crew safe.

Be awesome and buy Survival Mode direct from the author, with delivery by Bookfunnel.

ABOUT THE AUTHOR

Patty Jansen lives in Sydney, Australia, where she spends most of her time writing Science Fiction and Fantasy.

Her story *This Peaceful State of War* placed first in the second quarter of the Writers of the Future contest and was published in their 27th anthology. She has also sold fiction to genre magazines such as Analog Science Fiction and Fact, Redstone SF and Aurealis.

Patty has written over thirty novels in both Science Fiction and Fantasy, including the *Icefire Trilogy* and the *Ambassador* series.

pattyjansen.com

BOOKS BY PATTY JANSEN